THE
HAPPENING

An Experiment on Humankind

By Susan Varo

This is a story for all of those who see tomorrow.

CONTENTS

ACKNOWLEDGEMENTS

This book is dedicated to my loving and supportive parents, Mary and Robert Varo. I would like to give a special acknowledgment to my brother, Kevin Varo for suggesting the title for my book. I would like to give a big thank you to my mother, and to my friend Ana Rodriguez for their patience in taking the time to read my rough draft. Another thank you to my wonderful friend Elsie Plazza for supporting all of my crazy and important endeavors throughout the years, (God knows the laughs) and always remembering the things I have always aspired to do. Also, giving thanks to my sister, Lida Wallace and brother, Steve Varo for always listening to me constantly, regardless of what I have to say. Lastly, I'd like to thank my friends, Cecilia (Maria) Brindis, Casandra George, Wayne Coger, Elsie Plazza, Sr., Chantel Oates Salter, Stacey Smith and countless others who have all come through for me in very many ways. I am where I am, and who I am, thanks to all of you.

PREFACE

On the 25th of September in the fall of 1983, I was inspired by all of the technological changes in the world to write a book. It is a book about what I thought could occur in the future. With the use of foresight, and many of my premonitions, this is what I think could be happening. As mankind continues heading into the future, I have become frightfully aware of how technology may totally rule the world. It may, also, completely change the world as we know it.

As I wrote this book, I was at a lost as to a fitting title. I had talked with my brother Kevin, and I told him what the book would be about. He suggested calling it, "The Happening." He said it would be fitting, if such events could ever occur, events that could happen, or could well be happening right now. So, henceforth, I have given it this title.

As there are vast discoveries and improvements in current technology, future technology may be coming from various-unknown sources. I believe that there will be many new inventions unknown to many, but many of us will have been exposed. These inventions and discoveries may and can, unfortunately, be used in unconventional ways. They may be used to improve the many imperfections of the human race.

What could we do if inventors and scientists allow technology, and computers, to be responsible for the continued existence of men and women? What if this same technology were placed in the wrong hands? Some things should not be left to science, but rather to nature.

As I continued writing this book, I realized that, surely, there must be much more advanced technology that we would probably never know about that concerns our future. How strange it would be if the world we know, or think we know has, unabatedly, been altered through technology? What if it cannot, and will not be stopped, regardless of one's opposing feelings? Could there be a strange happening in the world that is happening right now?

PROLOGUE

When we examine the following powerful people, we can only imagine how important their lives must be, and the important decisions that they make. They must have a lot of responsibilities and must know how to delegate those responsibilities for specific purposes. For others like us, average citizens, the working class, should the following decisions made be the only decisions? What about the outcome of these decisions? What about the consequences we may all face?

Why and how did a simple-scientific experiment produce results, in such a way, that no one could ever explain? A scientific-cloning experiment designed for the elimination of viral, bacterial, and genetic diseases and various ailments that went wrong. Terribly wrong!

Let's just say that we have to further understand human nature. Then, maybe, we would understand that the purpose of bringing technology and scientific knowledge to fruition is to improve the way we live and improve mankind. It is, after all, better for us to advance and to further increase our knowledge so we can grow, and learn new ways to meet our full potential. We can learn this on a whole, as one race. The human race!

Sometimes scientists and those of higher authority can go too far and think of all sorts of ways to improve some imperfections of mankind. This is one of those bazaar instances based on scientific belief; whereas, scientists came up with the idea of using advanced-cloning techniques for the cure, and eradication of various diseases.

The idea is to select a human-diseased somatic cell, then separate the diseased portion of that cell by using energy and light-energy vibrations throughout the body. This is done during the cloning process.

The entire cell is then given specifically-engineered microantibodies and a technological-blue dye. The dye also illuminates within the cell and is sticky. It looks like blue water and is given by computer to an individual and can be given orally and topically. Along with this is a genetically-prepared solution, which causes any diseased portion of the cell to weaken. This process then spreads throughout the entire body, and begins working immediately on a deeper-cellular level. The diseased portion is then completely identified from the healthy part of the cell.

While the dye adheres to a cell, it also stains the cell making it clearly identifiable for experiments. It illuminates anywhere unhealthy conditions are present, whether on the surface of the skin, within muscle or deep inside bone.

When the microantibodies and solution come into contact with a healthy cell, a permanent-bonding occurs. The diseased portion is removed, and annihilated. The new genetically-illuminated cells, with the blue dye, continue cloning into healthy cells. These new cells continue replicating for the rest of the individuals life.

This technology is advantageous to any individual with any-particular ailment; as what has caused the illness is eradicated before the cell is cloned. Only healthy cells are recognized, and replicate into more healthy cells. Once a diseased cell is treated from a human being, nothing else needs to be done by that individual. This process begins on an individual lying on a bed during a physical examination, by a simple, 5th-dimensional, full-body scan. The scan sees various abnormalities: viruses, bacteria, energies, and diseases throughout the entire-human body.

The next process is called Living Photoscans, and the end result is an ongoing-cloning process. This is done entirely by computers to an individual. Although, done entirely by computers, a human technician and a medical helper are needed. They assist the computers while they are performing the cloning functions. The technician uses a device called a MCR or a Molecular Cellular Replicator. This device looks exactly like a hand-held mirror with a circular black center. It is made of a lightweight-gray polymer. It is eight inches in overall length, with a diameter of five inches. The MCR's entire outer-circular area tapers downward and forms the handle, which is held by the technician or helper. The circular-outer rim is an inch-and-a half wide from the darkened center, and two inches in thickness. The sunken-black center is called the Atometer. Although the entire MCR seems solid, the black center is not a solid area. Upon closer inspection, one can see a dizzying display of small dots bouncing off of each other. They are minuscule-energized atomic energy particles that appear dark, moving rapidly around in time and space. This is the area that is passed over an individual's body part that is being treated: an eye, ear or arm. Also, the area can be a foot, hair or any area where a cell needs to be cloned. When healthy replicated cells are taken, the process is done on such a small scale and scope, that it has to be magnified to be seen. It appears on a Screenview showing the actual interaction to the technician. The MCR sends light vibrations, blue dye and microantibodies, and light energy particles through the skin cells, to the bone, on a microscopic level. Then, it selects which cells it needs to use. A cell appears fibrous, where the energy particles have passed through each section.

Acquiring healthy cells do not involve physical extraction or disturbance or harm to the body. It is taking a living photograph that is replicated over and over. The treated cells are also held in the MCR's center, and can be given to another individual, or simply cloned at another time. It can also work the same for extracting healthy cells for cloning. Cells can also be placed into another body to replicate by being rubbed on in a lotion or spray. Nearly all of these methods can apply especially for young children.

Many adults who have undertaken this process have told others of an amazing side effect that they have received. After the process and experiencing the energy emitted, they report what they feel. It is an exhilarating, but temporary-electrical current flowing throughout their bodies, lasting on and off for several days. Many say it is an incredible, pseudo-sexual orgasm. It is an amazing experience and deemed a technological-sexual substitute without having the need of a partner. It is, quite frankly, something to remember for participation in the entire cloning experiment. Because of this, many volunteer themselves just to receive this pleasant-side effect.

This cloning treatment is, currently, only being used at a specific location. It is anticipated to be used on a grander scale and widespread throughout the world in medical practices.

CHAPTER 1

On October 20, 2024, The Duke Explorer Satellite Orbitor Surveyor returned to earth from its top-secret journey, throughout the far reaches of our galaxy. Its final destination was through the rings of Saturn. While traveling throughout the universe, it had been collecting microscopic-life forms and organisms to aid scientist on earth. This collection is for the creation of new-genetic cells for cloning.

A couple of months earlier on August 23rd, a renowned Astronomer, Harve Ryan discovered a mysterious, large, red-orange moon through his Shu Lampert's Digital-Optics Telescope. This moon had been orbiting Saturn. The profound discovery warranted an investigation, since scientists believed that there is life on this strange moon. The unmanned explorer, using its implanted-thought process had communications with a life force from this moon. It also sent data and light photoscan images back to earth. The incredible photoscans of the large moon, at times, could be seen in its entirety while at other times, appear as just a distorted image.

It also retrieved information that this orbiting moon has the capability of moving in and out of time and space within the universe. The data collected illustrates that there is life on this moon, which had also been seen orbiting very close to Jupiter. It had been masquerading as one of its twelve moons.

Scientists and researchers are baffled, and have gone to great lengths gathering data on this astronomical phenomenon. They think that this distortion is a way of it hiding itself, as it may have a hidden agenda.

The explorer had come into close proximity to this moon, and to its unknown atmosphere. It has come to be called Ryan's Moon, the name of its discoverer. The explorer had also intercepted and captured a probe that circled this moon. The probe seemed to have been collecting samples of materials emitted through space, and the effects of these materials on this moon and Saturn. It seemed to function like a recycling unit collecting information, and sending messages back to Ryan's Moon. The probe is completely alien, and does not consist of any known-earth materials. It is unlike anything made on earth.

When the explorer brought the probe to earth, a compartment is found within the probe that contained a large quantity of energized-crystal cells. The cells are analyzed, and are indeed found to be strange.

Some of the crystal cells had adhered themselves to the hull of the explorer, and have formed a rust-colored powered material. A few scientists believe that the heat of the explorer re-entering through the earth's atmosphere must have caused some chemical reaction, and thus the coloring.

These same scientists have named these energized-crystal cells Element G. Their properties are studied, and are found to be regenerative. They also have the capability of memory. When they are contained, they appear silvery like mercury, but have the consistency of gunpowder. They can be both a solid and a liquid, and are completely weightless.

There are many scientific debates about the origins of Element G, and various rumors have circulated. There is one scientist, who has speculated that it is an end product of human hemoglobin mixed with alien genetics, as if there was some sort of human experimentation done in the past.

Perhaps, this may be the case, thus given its rust-colored appearance on the hull. Also, it gives off an odd-energy field, which can be picked up by scanners and surveillance equipment over long distances. It can also be magnetized as well. Once exposed to the air or released from its' earthly containment, it becomes clear like bubbles, and changes shape and size.

It is extremely difficult to handle. When it collides with one another, it becomes semi-transparent, and changes into various-size cells like water droplets. It can also change texture, and all of these features may, in fact, be something needed for alien interactions.

The memory capability within these cells enables it to identify with its surrounding cells. It is assumed that these properties can be altered, if mixed with man-made or organic material. When a portion of it is extracted from the whole, it goes right back to the original portion, if placed within its vicinity, or beside it. If a portion of it is left on its own, it will multiply into a new and equal amount of cells, which it was originally separated.

It attracts to itself like a magnet, but has no metallic qualities. Also, due to its strange composition, it is held in high regards, because of its regenerative capabilities. It is thought to be best suited for use in cloning experiments; although, the long-term effects of its use have not yet been determined. It is believed that its regenerative capabilities can influence human cells to replicate, similarly, and quickly, and reproduce more healthy cells.

Other scientists believe that it has been created by an unknown-life form during some alien interaction. They believe the probe and this strange element will be recovered by some alien race. These cells react strangely to the earth's gravity. Since they are weightless, they continue to behave as though they are still within their celestial plane in space; therefore, they must be contained. If not, they will just float into the air like bubbles traveling through the atmosphere, and stratosphere back into outer space.

It has also been determined that Element G uses its magnetic capabilities, as a marker, to stay adhered to the Explorer. It must have known that the probe was within, and is why it didn't just float back into outer space, or Ryan's Moon.

The discovery of Ryan's Moon, which led to the discovery of Element G, however, was not Harve Ryan's alone. Unknown to anyone, there is one-solely responsible for the discovery. He happens to be Harve's assistant, Jim Harrison. He has not been included in this huge discovery, and feels hurt and betrayed. This has made him become disgruntled and vengeful.

On the evening of Thursday, August 22nd when Harve was not in the office, Jim had been in the observatory. He focused on an object in deep space through their Shu Lampert's Digital-Optics Telescope. He had to leave suddenly to go out of town, but left the telescope focused on the position where he saw the strange moon, orbiting the rings of Saturn. Since he would be unreachable, and not back in the office for several days, he decided to leave a note. It is written for Harve to read the following morning. Being unable to tell Harve personally, he made sure the message was very detailed. He then taped it on top of Harve's desk.

They share a nicely-designed office space in a beautifully-constructed building. They work together at The Cosmic Observatory, located within a two-acre section of land, in the San Bernardino Valley. This solar-powered observatory adjoins an office building, and university. It is where many in the scientific community come to work, and study. It is housed in a reinforced, bright-white concrete base that is covered by a dome made from layers of lenses of blue-transparent steel. When in operation, the dome opens at the top, from opposite sides by four-individual overlapping and transitional-layered lenses. Each is filled with a copper-colored infrastructure. These layered-lenses project outward and downward for skyward viewing. The outer lenses are discreetly covered with solar panels.

Over the years, Harve and Jim have encountered many hardships and had been unable to make any significant discoveries. Harve being older and more experienced has more knowledge of scientific information, which includes people and places that he has never shared. This has always beleaguered Jim. They have had many personal conflicts, and their working relationship has been strained. Harve has lost his zest for life and physically, he has just let himself go. His bad hygiene and ever-growing protuberance irks Jim so much, that he continuously nags him to take care of himself. Jim tries to maintain a professional-working relationship, and had hoped that something would happen to bridge their professional and personal-relationship gap.

Harve returns the next morning on August 23rd and reads the incredible message. He knows what a tremendous discovery this is and menacingly, decides to take full credit for it. He observes the moon through the telescope, and has since been known to have made this amazing discovery.

Jim arrives back in the office a few days later on August 28th, and excitedly asks Harve, "Did you see the note I left?" Harve looks at him deviously and answers, "What note?" Jim stares at him a little confused and in disbelief and replies: "I left you a written message! Gee, I hope the cleaning staff didn't remove it, and toss it in the trash. There is a moon near Saturn… didn't you get it?"

He studies Harve for a moment reading his face, and gets a deep-sinking feeling in his stomach. He feels numb, and starts to think that something troubling has begun. He motions with his head, as if Harve will give up his secret, and also to see if he is joking. Having already surmised that Jim is onto him, he knows there is going to be trouble. Harve mentally completes a plan that will determine Jim's fate. He says: "I didn't see a note, but I just want to let you in on a little secret. I have already told nearly everyone in the astronomy and scientific community, and major universities, that I have made this incredible discovery."

Jim is stunned to say the least and says: "I've only been gone for a few days, and you've done all of this without me? How did all of this happen so fast?" He glares at Harve in disbelief with a look of astonishment on his face. Before he can utter a word, Harve begins: "I will be away for a couple of months on conference in regards to the discovery. During this time that I am away from the observatory, I will be meeting with scientists and astronomers to discuss the discovery, which will be kept from the general public. This moon is unlike any other, and we all want to be sure of what it truly is before making any announcements. They and I will not be reachable so, you'll have to hold down the fort."

As Jim is about to confront Harve, their office door quickly opens and in walks their supervisor, Dave Maggens. Without any recognition to Jim, he asks Harve, "Are you ready to go?" Jim interrupts: "I think we need to have a discussion about this. I was a part of this and why haven't I been acknowledged?" Dave looks at him and replies: "What part of this have you been involved in?" Jim answers: "I discovered it! I was away and told Harve before I left." Dave asks, "Harve is that true?" He answers: "Not at all! Jim was away and I told him about it." Dave asks: "Jim, why did you leave if you knew of this and didn't bring it to my attention?" Jim replies: "I had to help a friend who had an emergency. She and I, well, it's complicated were trying to resolve a situation from the past; I stayed out of touch for a few days." Dave asks: "Well, how do you want me to rectify this now? The scientific community believes that Harve is the discoverer and preparations have already been made." Jim gasps and yells, "Tell them the truth!" Dave asks, "Jim can you prove it? Jim replies: "Yes, I wrote a note and it should be stored in the surveillance in this room…" Harve interrupts and says: "The note only said you'd be away a few days and nothing more." Jim becomes upset and this puts Dave in an awkward position so he asks: "Harve are you telling me the truth?" He responds, "Yes, of course!" Jim tries his best to be convincing but cannot offer any proof. Dave says to both of them: "We'll have to straighten this out later. There are too many people waiting. Jim, are you coming with us?" He replies angrily: "Why? What am I supposed to say? Will you tell everyone that it was me and not Harve?" Dave answers: "I cannot prove

9

it or change the arrangements already made. We have to leave now. Jim, I'll get back to you later." This leaves Jim all alone in the office in a fury. He realizes he has been totally ignored in what could be the greatest discovery of all time. Jim resigns to the fact that this may alter his future and what may become of him now.

A month passes, and it is now September. Jim is still working in the office he shares with Harve, but he's unhappy. As what used to make him happy has become the doldrums of working in an office. Throughout the month, he is consumed with thoughts of everything that he does and how it may never compare to what Harve may have accomplished. Sickened by his lack of involvement and unable to manage to follow in Harve's pursuits, he works on other tasks waiting to see what will come his way. Also, in Harve's absence, he tries to learn of his whereabouts and what may be taking place well into the middle of October.

On October, 30, 2024, Harve returns back to the observatory and to his office. He finds Jim busy at his desk. Harve looks happy and content while Jim looks up with a scowl and anger. Harve asks, "What have you been up to?" Jim glares at him as if he is a total stranger. Then Harve asks, "Have you heard the latest?" Jim replies almost inaudibly: "I don't know what you're talking about."

Harve goes on to say: "I have been informed by a group of scientists, many of whom have heralded my amazing discovery, upon the Duke Explorer's return to earth, that it collected a strange-unknown material. Didn't you watch and listen to the scientific reports? The material has been named Element G. It has been found to have some very, very strange and otherworldly-extraterrestrial properties that may be an incredible boon to mankind. They and I have sworn to secrecy that we would not discuss the Element G part with anyone. I have been told that it is going to be integrated into industrial and everyday household products, and so forth. It has metallic qualities, its lead free for all we know, never rusts or expires. The major use of it will be for medicinal purposes. Since genealogy is the largest, and one of the most important and widely-funded medical establishment that currently exists, many hope it is where it will prove to be most useful."

Jim bites his lip in anger and asks like before: "How did all of this happen so fast?" Harve continues: "You know how quickly science works today, and there is a place that's equipped to handle all of this." He starts to talk about this place, and where Element G is secretly being housed. He says slyly: "You should learn about D.U.G. pronounced Doug, as it's called." He presents a long, translucent, and wafer-thin blueprint screen of DUG's entire complex, and places it on a desk. Jim half heartily looks at it without a word. Having this

11

inside information makes Harve feel powerful, as he rubs it in Jim's face. Harve has become greedy, and feels that this is what he has worked for all of his life. Also, it gives him the chance to finally be free of Jim.

Harve has no intention of sharing this discovery with anyone. He is very serious, and makes it clear that he is taking full credit for this tremendous discovery. Jim is completely aware of Harve's ruthless intentions, and in his infuriation lunges at him. This sends Harve scurrying backwards, and throwing his arms up in defense. Jim makes a fist, and swings into mid-air very close to Harve's face. He steps backwards, and realizes in his fury that Harve will never admit the truth. He will have to somehow prove that he was a part of the discovery.

It is almost as unbearable, as it is unbelievable. Jim walks towards him, biting his lip, and blurts out with fury: "What? You did what? How? Without me! You bastard, I told you about this. We work together, we're a team. You could have at least mentioned my name. Come on, say something!" Harve replies dryly: "No, it's too late. It's already done. I can't change the story of the discovery now. Who'd believe it?" Jim breathes heavily and yells out, "Son of a bitch!" Harve becomes afraid and backs away, but bumps loudly into his desk. He loses his balance and falls backwards grabbing the desk behind him to keep from falling to the floor. Jim lunges at him, and punches him square on his left cheek. He tumbles off the side of the desk, and hits the floor with a thud.

In the scuffle, the blueprint blows off the desk, and into the air. It glides back and forth for a few moments, and falls to the floor landing softly by the door. Jim stands hunched with his legs spread apart, waiting for Harve to retaliate. Dazed and frightened, Harve grabs his jaw and struggles to pick himself up. Jim hovers over him and says: "You backstabber! I'll get you for this. Mock my words, I'll get you, you son of a bitch!"

Jim slowly backs off, and regains his composure, and begins taking his personal belongings from the office. He gets a large, black-garbage bag from a closet, and throws everything he can inside of it. He grabs his jacket, and the DUG blueprint off the floor, and storms out of the office. Harve staggers towards the door, and foolishly and maliciously calls behind him, "Jim! Wait!" With a weak an evil chuckle he blurts out: "Why don't you go to DUG, where you can work with part of the discovery, and Element G? Tell them I sent you." There is no response from Jim, as he hurries along his way. After gathering his wits, Harve looks down the hall to see if he is gone. When he turns back, he realizes he has been careless, and Jim has taken the blueprint. He only wanted to taunt him with it, but now there is nothing he can do to stop him.

Sometime later, Jim arrives home, still infuriated with not being recognized for the amazing discovery. This leaves him only one choice. He knows that Harve will never admit that he didn't make the discovery alone. He knows what he has to do and devises a plan. Knowing that he can no longer trust or work with Harve again, he figures out a way where he could still be part of the discovery, and get even with Harve. He looks over the blueprint, and remembers Harve mentioning Element G. He starts thinking about how he will find it, and how to misuse it. With the blueprint in his possession, nothing can stop him. He has knowledge, and he also has power.

On November 18, 2024, Jim manages to join DUG, also known as Development Underground using the blueprint. He's ecstatic, and starts out as a scientist assistant learning about Element G.

Having the blueprint from Harve, he also has some clout, and because of this knowledge, there is concern as to what else he may know. The facility won't risk letting him go, and risk any security implications that may arise of him working elsewhere. Unbeknownst to anyone, there will be a price to pay when he joins, and the cost is quite high.

14

DUG has been around for quite some time. Its purpose is to mine natural elements from the earth, using advanced-technological principals. This is done by removing minerals and other naturally-occurring elements from various mines and fields without depleting, or causing any environmental damage. This establishment has become integrated with individuals from scientific, medical, scholastic, and industrial backgrounds to create ways of harnessing the earth's riches.

When an area is harnessed for its riches, it is cordoned off, and technologically treated. It is left to regenerate, over a short time, to be mined again. It has become such a successful operation it needed to expand. To do so, it has continuous access to farther and deeper regions of the earth.

In order to keep this establishment running so well, and so organized, it keeps its workers in line on a continuous basis. People are taken here willingly and unwillingly, for work and human-mutation engineering. Their mutated cells are then sent to other establishments to assist with a specific type of process for cloning.

It can be an unsettling place, where all parts of the body are developed beyond their normal usage. There are specimens, with the help of technology that have learned to use their vision beyond its normal capabilities. Their irises and pupils appear mechanical, and have leeched into some of the sclera, of both eyes. Others are capable of hearing well beyond normal-human range, and some whose heads are deformed due to their enormous cerebral capacity and use.

These unique individuals are given natural and synthetic-technological materials allowing them to enhance their capabilities. Many have had what is natural in appearance altered. Other things such as appetite and sleep patterns are altered. Their appearance has changed to resemble another form of being. These unique individuals then become employees, and perform tasks that no average human being can accomplish.

These employees perform duties with limited amounts of sleep, minimal amounts of nutrition, and with unlimited energy. When they reach this level, they are perfect candidates for cloning. They are also coupled off, and their children have these similar and other extraordinary qualities. This is a lucrative establishment, and there is a lot to be gained. These individuals are exchanged for information and power from other locales, and are part of a large import and export service.

There is one individual here named Normus. He began working here in January 2024, and stands six-feet five inches tall, and he's huge. He is kept in a specific laboratory, where experimental Element G is now housed, and unknowingly leaking from the rim of a glass container. Normus, a previously healthy man, suffered a terrible-vehicle accident, and sustained a head injury. With mind and brain developing experiments, he is fully rehabilitated.

Normus has developed mental capabilities to withdraw huge amounts of technological information by mentally linking itself to networks, and systems throughout the complex.

Everything created here has value that can be exchanged for another form of compensation. This operation is completely underground and spreading worldwide. Once someone has any knowledge of it, they can be killed, or are used for their knowledge. They must join willingly, and never disclose their knowledge to anyone. It is a very high price to pay either way.

Within this underground-based laboratory, there is a very powerful and mysterious man who is in charge of this enormous facility. His name is Captain Meyers, and he has a huge amount of authority. He is a striking man: tall, well made with thick brows, and a strong nose. He has deep-set eyes, which has a dizzying effect upon one, and a demeanor that reveals one whom carries many secrets.

DUG is stationed in San Diego, in a secluded location that is partially a desert that descends deeply underground. It is equipped to dig deep for oil, diamonds, ore, and other natural elements. It also transports organic goods of every kind underground; as there are so few natural elements left, being dug from above ground.

Its existence is kept secret, and its entrance is located below a tall, white, spacious-office building. On one side of this office building is a very faint, flashing, purple-chevron sign accompanied by a low-repetitive tone, which signify all personnel to its secret location. Those who work outside of this development don't express any interest or curiosity in the chevron. It has subliminally pre-programmed them to work amongst themselves. The building workers succumb to the tones that are played continuously, when they enter and leave. The tones causes these workers to perform like worker bees and no questions are asked and they just get to work. Those that are not DUG workers, never interfere with DUG or their comings or goings.

Those who work here are conditioned to remain loyal employees to this underground dwelling through fear. They are continuously exposed to the effects of a MCR while working. This offers them a much welcomed pseudo-sexual side effect, which helps many tolerate being on the job.

The various laboratories located here are only a small part of this operation. It is also a manufacturing plant that makes computer components: lightweight-durable metals, and universally-compatible software that it secretly exports worldwide. It also has its own government. There is no other place like it on earth.

It supplies every known element, and communication device ever developed, and more. It houses materials gathered from space missions. It is also where transparent steel is made exclusively, and the ingredients are an extremely, closely-guarded secret. It is also solar powered which is advantageous, as it receives filtered sunlight in every area. Most of the materials manufactured here are grown from crystals. These crystals are formed from various materials: glass, metals, liquids and solids. They are fused with cosmic materials to create new materials, with unimaginable capabilities.

DUG is an engineering marvel, and it is a living laboratory. It is constructed like a fortress. Many of the scientists who work here live here. The few outsiders who know of this secret location consider it to be the eighth wonder of the world.

There is no communication within the entire complex, in the conventional manner by workers to their families. They do not see their families, and communicate only through cellular-molecular communication. This communication is done by an acutely sensitive honeycombed-shaped wafer implanted inside the ear on the cochlea, and auditory nerve. When in use, it branches out and filters down to the back of the throat, where one can just whisper to be heard.

Many sensitive individuals have learned to use their extra-sensory perception. They send signals to their families mentally, or to their home Screenviews, where signals can be picked up directly by the receiver.

A Screenview is a finely-woven energy screen, where one can watch programs or participate in any particular event. There are two types of Screenviews, and either can be used for home or work. The first type is one that is created within a room from a central-energy field. It occupies space and time, but is not contained in a structure, nor is it a surface. It cannot be fully seen until a program is being viewed. It then becomes a full-color viewing area for showing programs. It works with invisible-energized vibrating particles that receive messages and images sent through the air, and other sources. Each individual particle is designed to change size, color, shape and dimension to accommodate any program. It's on a whole-new level of technology.

When turned on and there are no programs being displayed, Screenview resemble that of dust particles floating around in a sun's ray coming through a window.

The images within this technological mesh are crystal clear, and can be seen on either side. Someone can actually walk around, and through this energy screen, as it is not tangible. It captures an image like a movie screen did in the past, but places it into a dimensional state. It does not need to be projected upon, or within anything. It can be seen anywhere, within a room or area. It can be right in front of the viewer, or thirty feet away.

The second type of Screenview can be superimposed upon an object or objects. For example, it can cover a window, and the window can become the screen. While the window is still a solid object, it is transformed by the Screenview, and becomes a viewing surface. When one is finished with Screenview it can simply be turned off, and the window and its surrounding views are restored to normal.

Only those associated with DUG, and certain family members use this particular technology for communication, and no one is allowed to speak of it.

DUG is fully equipped with a private-banking system, greenhouse, water supply, and gravitational field. It also has an energy field, and a magnetic-energy field. All of the water that supplies this underground world comes from a private reservoir. The water-filtering system has a recycling system. It also regenerates-filtered sunlight, and can recreate artificial sunlight.

It has its own clothier, medical establishment, library, and communication stations. It has a railway system that is incomparable to any other. The railway system trains can easily reach speeds up to 165 miles-per-hour, which moves its workers from place to place, and is completely silent. Trains entering the many stations below ground have platforms on both sides, allowing passengers to enter, and exit from either side. There are no rails or wheels, and it travels within the platform. From station-to-station it is atop a flat, six-foot wide transparent-steel surface that goes on for miles.

This surface sits on a bed that is masterfully constructed and lightweight and made of transparent steel. It rolls out on a magnetic, treadmill-pulley system. There are many of these pulleys that extend for miles. They transport the trains moving above like one, enormous, conveyor-belt-of ingenuity. Its concept is based on a scroll design, and works perfectly. When the train leaves the station, the pulley system stops and waits for the next approaching train. The train picks up enormous speed, and literally rides on air. The platform also serves as a conduit for electricity, while it's transporting.

Below where the train sits within the platform, on either side are walls that have large and round, evenly-spaced holes. These holes travel the entire distance of the platform throughout the railway system. Water pours out from these holes, onto the steel surface beneath the train.

On the underside of the train is a flat, steel-pulley surface similar to the surface below it. Water flowing from these holes, collects and pools upon these two-steel surfaces. This allows the train to glide forward, or backward, while moving or in the station. The water and steel, along with the energy field, generates electricity. The magnetic field and the water prevent the two surfaces from actually touching, and the train can steadily move in either direction. The combination makes for a smooth-comfortable ride. The processed currents of electricity also provide additional power for the solar-powered systems; this creates more regenerated power for lighting within the trains and the stations.

Everything works in cycles, and nothing is wasted. The system is basically foolproof, and there is practically no maintenance required. As long as there is water, a magnetic field and gravity, the system works. This technology has also been built into the West Coast Rail System.

A large part of California's new 160-foot wide airway-rail system uses DUG technology. It runs on a single, and continuous transparent steel, and glass-beam platform. It is dazzling in the sunlight, and it stretches for thousands of miles. It shines like melting ice, and is incredibly strong. Its fusing with steel crystals gives it its strength, and glass crystals give it its appearance.

Although strong and transparent, it is lightweight and supported from below every several-hundred feet, by perfectly-shaped-gleaming spiral arches. The arches are surrounded by clear-tubular structures. With a systematic-gravitational field, it is also flexible and buoyant. It can bend, which makes it suitable for various weather, and climatic conditions. It is made purposely to suit California's vulnerability to earthquakes.

Trains travel along this glass-rail system at top speeds, with virtually no sound at all. The passengers inside feel they are truly riding on air. If there is an earthquake, the system can support itself for miles, because of the glass and steel and special ingenuity that is built into it.

Between each spiral arch are sensors for such an event. If too many arches are destroyed due to natural disaster, an energy field takes over. This buffers the railway for a very long period of time, while suspending it in the air. Like a spiral staircase, it is supported amongst itself. These combinations form a pattern of unimaginable tensile strengths.

At DUG, there are no cameras, security guards, or locks on doors. It is a living and interactive location. Everything is based on simple principles and physics. Inside the walls, and floors are water canals. Once someone enters the underground location, they are monitored for life.

An unseen arch is built above all the entrance doorways, throughout the complex, with a device called Scan Invisible. The entrance appears like any other doorway to a room, but it takes a scanned blueprint image of the entire body from head to toe. The scanned information stays in the establishment permanently. Everything from ethnicity, illness to DNA is obtained in a nanosecond.

An unsuspecting person would have no clue that this is taking place. Anything foreign that enters is also scanned, whether an insect, dust, sound or energy. This also includes a change of temperature to cigarette smoke, as nothing can get past the system.

Authorized personnel are already subjected to this scan upon initiation, and are detected anywhere throughout the complex. They are only re-scanned if there are physiological or mental changes from the original scan. Scan Invisible remembers each and every individual, and they become part of the system, and are seen as part of a whole. You can say man, woman and machine become one. There is no privacy within this complex. The walls, technically, do have eyes, ears and more.

If there were ever to be a dangerous individual, or object that enters, the water canals housed in the walls, floor and ceiling activate. It is so incredibly sensitive that the direction of the individual, or object, is instantaneously calculated by the flow of water in the floor under their feet. To the individual, the floor and walls are solid. The movement of the water indicates the direction the individual is heading. When the individual gets to a location where he or she can be contained, the water moving below their feet joins and pools with the water in the walls. The water flowing above in the ceiling stops over the doorway, as gravity quickly pulls down a hidden door from above. Thus, sealing one's fate until that individual is released.

The biggest secret about DUG is it's actually in plain sight, in an ordinary, 10-story, white-office building. The upper and lower floors are only accessible to DUG workers. Once a DUG worker enters the building, they head for the elevator bank at the rear, along with the building workers. They are led down to another-world underground using an adjourning set of rotating elevators. No one has ever suspected anything unusual, and its workers appear like the other building workers. Many are never seen again because they will live here. Others come back out on rare occasions.

They are all completely separated from society, as we know it. There are some DUG workers deemed, The Clockwise Workers, because they do not live here, but have different shifts. They use the rotating elevators each day. The workers are called this, as what they do is taken in the literal sense. When a Clockwise worker enters the front elevator to start their shift, the doors open and then close. The back doors of the front elevator open leading to the back elevator. These doors then open and close and the worker heads downward underground. This leaves the front elevator ready for use. The elevators are actually, two-separate elevators joined together. The one in the front is for the building workers, and the one in the back is for DUG workers. They're two, equal-size cubes latched onto each other perfectly to form one-large elevator. Also, they can actually rotate around each other. It functions on a magnetic-pulley system, within a state-of-the art tramway system.

The elevator system works well, offering speed, consistency, great security and anonymity for the workers. When building workers and clockwise workers both enter the elevator at the same time, there is a faux-top floor that the building workers never use. The clockwise worker goes up to this floor, then enters the back elevator, and then goes underground. They clock in and do their assignment, and at the end of the day clock out. They take the back elevator back up to the top floor, or whatever floor the empty-front elevator is located and connects, and then goes downward to the main floor picking up the other building workers. The cycle continues, and there is no mix up.

There are no buttons, or floor numbers on these elevators just sensors. A Scan Invisible is applied here, as well. All workers are taken to their designated locations, because they are scanned in the system from the beginning, as to where they are assigned. The building workers are always taken to their destinations first, so they don't see the other workers enter the back bank of elevators. Also, these workers have no reason to socialize with one another. It is a successful operation.

Universal Software is created here, which has infinite uses such as in Screenviews, computers, music equipment, and appliances. It also creates transportation equipment, prosthetics, medical facilities, and so many other products, and devices.

Highly Sensitive Devices or HSD's are a very small part of the software. It is activated by heat, light, energy and movement. It records, reads programs and data, and retains information simultaneously. It performs in a sequence by assimilating its environment. It operates within a vacuum in its surroundings to accumulate vast amounts of information. It has the ability to accommodate distance and area. It is a portal of information. There are minute grids, within minute grids designed within a HSD. The sequences of grids enable information to be extracted and stored into one grid at a time with incredible speed. Energy, heat levels, and various colors of light encompass one area. The information becomes activated upon contact. This can be from a living individual, or a form of technology. Bands of a color spectrum can be retrieved to receive thousands, upon thousands of bits of information, which can be used in various ways at one time. They are so highly sensitive; they do not require assistance for usage. Once an energy source comes into contact with it, massive amounts of information can be extracted, or become readily available. One can actually hold a HSD in their hand, and activate it into many uses. Whether it involves sights, sounds or information, this can be performed straight from a HSD. An individual's energy can be pulled in as well. That energy can be sent to a source such as playing music on a device, or sent to another type of communication device. It's an incredible type of technology in a small space. It works as a thought process taken to the extreme. Colors can be projected onto other objects, just from an individual's energy. This technology is basically creating individual-dimensional reality on a wavelength, on a sub-anatomic particle scale. It is best to use compatible-sensitive devices of communication to handle the capabilities of this type of technology. Universal software is taking intangible technology and bringing it to life. Now one can physically hold, interact and experience their environment, and the entire world.

This type of technology has a monopoly over everything, and is governed onto itself. This is all possible, as there are no strongholds of any super powers, including the United States Government that can interfere, as it is no more. Nor is there any other governing agency that could intercede. The United States Government has been broken down into various structures, which handle specialized aspects within society. The president and members of the cabinet, statesmen, and the like are assigned into leveled branches of common and diplomatic affairs. There are various-other authorities in power that handle matters from medical facilities, military, housing, and scientific communities throughout the world. There is a continuously growing, and ongoing process of delegation of power within these many authorities that seem nearly unimaginable.

Since there is so much technological power, it has taken control of daily life. It has changed the dynamics, and structure of how governing the populous has been done decades earlier. Most citizens have acquired what was previously unobtainable intelligence, and it doesn't serve much more than a hot topic. Nearly everything is integrated, and this puts everyone on similar levels.

CHAPTER 2

Over the next three months, in February 2025, Jim Harrison is placed in a position as a technician. As luck would have it, he will also be working with Element G. Unbeknownst to him, he is assigned to a specific room at DUG by Captain Meyers. The captain will be instructing him on the usage of Element G. The captain also has sophisticated knowledge on how to use a MCR to utilize Element G for various uses.

From the onset of Jim's arrival, the captain takes an immediate liking to him joining his team. Unfortunately, he takes Jim under his wing, and passes along his sophisticated knowledge, while training and molding his new apprentice. He teaches Jim how to use the properties of Element G to experiment with known-earth materials. He learns how to add it to previously separated liquids, and solids of various-organic materials. He also learns how to bind it to other broken-down atomic elements. Jim cannot understand how the captain could know so much about a newly-discovered material. Many scientists and geneticists have not been able to definitively analyze what it truly is. Somehow, he feels compelled to comply with the captain's request, and he seems to have no control of his decisions. He also notices something about the captain that he has never experience with any other human being before.

There is something very deep, and sinister that shows in the captain's vacant expression. His eyes are hollow, and Jim can see through the openings of his pupils. He's solid as a person, but there's nothing within the living-breathing individual. There is absolutely no emotion or soul. It's as if he just exists, but only because there is some driving force that is helping him. He also senses something odd, and even otherworldly that he can't quite put his finger on. He has a deep sense of dread. It's as though someone or something is preventing him from reacting to the captain's strangeness, by not allowing his emotions towards the captain to surface. It doesn't seem to matter; as he believes, he will finally have infinite power to get even with Harve Ryan. It is what he has been waiting for. He will forever be indebted to the captain for his new position, and for being his powerful-secret ally.

Jim will collect Element G, using a MCR that will be used in a large room where he is assigned. The room has a dimensional, wall-size energy screen that can see into the assembly room. His workstation is within this room that is made mostly of glass, and has every upscale amenity imaginable. It is universally equipped with a laboratory, experiment platform, eating room and Screenview. All of the equipment he needs is at his disposal, and he is at liberty to use all of it at his leisure. The assembly room is alongside Jim's room, but it is a separate laboratory. This is the area where computer parts are being created and assembled. Since Element G has the ability to move in and out of time and space, and has the capability of memory, he can just send a command with his MCR. This command sends Element G's cells away from the MCR, which goes to an assembly machine. Element G, along with its alien properties, then binds with the molecules that go into a working computer. Once a part is completed, it is sent to be added to the final product. There are various parts that Jim will work with. He is told by the captain that an experimental-cloning computer is being assembled, and he may see some of the actual parts while working within the assembly area. He is also told not to be concerned, as it won't pertain to him. He need not have any part in the assembly. Unfortunately for the captain, Jim is harboring dark thoughts. Jim believes this computer could bring him notoriety and finally success in the discovery of Element G.

Within the next three months, in May 2025, Jim has become accustomed to the routine of his new position, and the operations at DUG. At this time, the parts for the new computer come into the assembly room, but a few parts are mistakenly sent to Jim. He is ecstatic, and has no fear for the ramifications of his devious intent. The mix up was incredibly easy to make.

Since this is his area, there is no need for concern, and he just needs to pass the parts along accordingly. He now has the means for his motives. He has thought of many ways to use Element G in unsafe, and hazardous environments, and in products that have not yet been fully tested for compatibility.

Jim has already considered placing it in parts of various modes of transportation, and building materials that should not be engineered together. He also has thoughts of sinisterly engineering it into materials, in areas that would cause a weak support. This includes buildings and various constructions: railroads, bridges, as well as heavy metals, and plastics. Since its' safety has not been completely standardized in some materials, Jim feels, it can give him an edge towards his goal.

During this time, Normus is found dead lying on the floor in his laboratory, after only being employed from January 2024 through April 2025. Unfortunately, during one process, he mentally accessed the wrong information, and was exposed to some formatted-electrical stimulation. His brain and nervous system had shut down. When medical staff removed his body, they are frightened by a lingering, black-shapeless form in a far corner of the room. They are startled, and don't know what to do. The dark form slowly moves towards them, as if recognizing the lifeless body on the floor. It then glides across to the other side of the room, and disappears. A male staff member then murmurs, "Could that have been Normus' spirit?" A female staff member replies: "I don't know, but we better tell the captain." The body is taken to be examined, and an investigation begins.

Within the next several days, Jim calmly incorporates Element G into the circuitry, and visual aspects of the cloning-computer components using his MCR. He will be largely responsible for whatever happens after using Element G, which will also be used at The Laboratory and Research Organization building located in Sacramento, California. This is his revenge against Harve and he wants to truly make him pay for not acknowledging him in this monumental discovery. He's determined to disgrace Harve's name. If he can prove that only harmful events have arisen since the discovery, he would be victorious. In time, the fruits of his labor will provide both.

Over the next few weeks, strange events have begun to occur at DUG, as Jim continues to work with Element G. At various times, witnessed by many workers throughout the complex are tiny, semi-transparent round objects seen floating about from ceiling to floor. These objects appear as silvery balls of mercury. Sometimes, they are in groups that float around, and then they disperse, and quickly disappear. Staff members in various locations of the complex try to capture the objects for analysis, but they completely disappear, as if shut off by a switch. There have also been sightings of a dark-shadowy mass moving throughout various laboratories. Also, at this time, Normus death investigation is complete, and the cause of death is unknown. His cellular decomposition is deemed abnormal. There has been a mutation of cells and some behaving like the properties of Element G; yet, other cells remain unknown.

Scientists and technicians, working within the laboratories, believe that these objects are part of an experiment. It could, possibly, be the spirit of a deceased-experimental human that had gone wrong. Rumors have begun circulating that Normus is haunting the facility. The truth is, in fact, that these objects are Element G. They are looking for what they were once a part of, and are searching for their place of origin. Since the cells are being incorporated with earthly materials, they are unwillingly, beginning to integrate. Normus had been exposed to Element G, and its essence is trapped trying to connect with the cells, creating a fifth-dimensional state. Not dead or alive, but transformed.

Jim is totally aware from what he has learned from the captain that these cells have the capability of memory tracking, and monitoring each other throughout deep regions of outer space. Like moths attracted to a flame, they will unabatedly, try to go to what attracts them. They seem to be searching for something, possibly, their moon. He knows that these tiny cells are super intelligent, and that they form an energy chain that can exceed far from this underground laboratory. They can communicate through interstellar space, and carry energy networks that function like transmitters of yesteryear. It is like envisioning copper wires attached to two-tin cans, but over trillions of miles. If these crystal cells escape into the atmosphere, they will travel into deep space, and back to their origin. They'll behave like millions of tiny balloons filled with helium, released on a windy day. They function on a whole, but this pattern has been disrupted.

It is Thursday, May 29, 2025 and situated in a section of Sacramento, California stands a large-laboratory building in an area called Las Tierras. The building is clearly defined with black-serif letters that read, Laboratory and Research Organization. It is just off a long stretch of highway, where there is a quiet-little town below. It covers an area of three-city blocks in size, including its surrounding landscape, and is a strange sight to see. It has but a few, small, dark-rectangular windows and just eight floors. Each room in the laboratory has one window where sunlight or moonlight may enter. Some workers inside the laboratory are fortunate enough to have a window that faces the sun. Others work in subdued lighting, with artificial light on the other side of the building.

On some evenings, when the moon is full, its light enters through the windows on dazzling, bluish-white moon beams. Angling downwards, they crawl gingerly across the floor. Only those fortunate enough to work a late night can appreciate this.

The façade and entire surface of the building is highly iridescent, and shines with a red-orange bluish hue. On days when the sun is very bright, the reflection from the building can actually hurt the eyes to look upon it. Its color and design play upon the eyes the way one might see the sun shining upon the ocean, with the same bright, and sparkling-effects radiating off the water's surface. It is designed to repel curious onlookers. On days when there is no bright sun or it's cloudy, there is an all-around feeling of impending doom. Structurally, it has a menacing quality that quietly resonates beware. It is a way to protect the workers inside, who want their work to be kept as secretive as possible.

The entrance is at one side of the building to further provide extra security. Workers have to pass by the front of the building for access. There is also a separate underground-garage ramp that leads onto the highway. Most workers use the garage, and others use the walkway to get to the nearest transportation to get a ride. The garage is another security measure to keep the workers vehicles out of view, and safe.

The building is another high-tech, universally-equipped development, and is protected continuously. Like DUG, it has its own self-containing facilities. There is no visible surveillance anywhere, and only authorized personnel can enter. Those who do not work here, and approach the area, feel a strange and ominous presence. This prohibits close contact. It is to dissuade anyone who may be passing along from the highway, and are curious about this strange site. This presence is powerful and highly successful. The workers are immune to the odd effects surrounding the building, which emit constant-hypnotic disorientation upon everyone, or anything else.

Even though this type of security is in place, there is one real guard on duty named Mannie. It patrols for only a few hours in the morning, before workers arrive. It leaves, only to return for a couple of hours in the afternoon, before workers leave to go home. It is not there much longer after that. This is only to keep an eye on the workers, or address any issues that arise. It makes sure that they safely enter, and leave the building.

Most workers never give Mannie a second thought in regards to security. They feel the building is enough protection. But unlike any other security guard, Mannie is a rare-genetic mishap that was caused by the merging of chromosomes. It has turned Mannie into a combination of not quite man, and not quite woman. It is termed fusion, neither male nor female. Its lifetime identification will always be fusion, never mister or miss.

Mannie has very plain features, a neutral point of view, and an almost-sullen personality. When not on duty, this is the only time it is a concern for the building, if an intruder were to try to enter. It would be due to an extreme case someone finds a vulnerable way of entry; Mannie is there to oversee it all. It would be due to an extreme weakness or malfunction in the security system. These are particular times that are of concern. It is not too often, but it does occur that a worker leaves early.

Once all workers are inside, there is no need for a guard between business hours. It is completely cost effective, and there is no salary paid for more guards. It is a well-thought-out system.

Surrounding most of the building complex is a fence, with a thick hedge grown into it. It blocks out most of the view of the small town below. The outer-surrounding landscape slopes down into more overgrown shrubs, which give way to the highway. Being near traffic, no one has yet tried to trespass upon this eerie site. It is an area where everyone keeps his or her distance.

All of those who work here have sworn to secrecy that they would never discuss, or bring any of their business outside of the building. No work can be brought home for completion, and no aspects are mentioned about what they do. The law protects all of the workers; if they are caught betraying it in any way, the law will provide punishment. This is an oath they must take to their graves. The workers and their work are always tracked. It's the job of the employee-print tracking disk to sense where a worker is at all times. The security system detects any important objects, or materials moved, used or taken throughout the laboratory.

At the tip of each finger, implanted beneath the skin of all workers, is an oval-clear disk. This painless implantation is done at the beginning of employment as a safeguard, in case an employee has damage done to their hands due to experiments. The disks are a copy of the natural imprint of the finger. It is also an invisible-tracking system. The workers are also integrated in the buildings-employment system, so the fingertips are only a small piece of the identification process.

Along with natural fingerprints left on items throughout the laboratory by workers, the computer-generated fingerprints are left behind as well. When any item is picked up in the laboratory, and moved from place to place, both sets of prints are tracked and monitored continuously. An item can always be detected, whether missing, misplaced or stolen by the print tracking.

If a worker used instruments or items that are no longer in their possession, the disk prints are tracked until those items are returned to their original location. These prints are monitored no matter where, he or she may be in the world. Materials such as tubes and various solutions are also monitored by how long they are removed from their shelves, or containment locations. Any material not detected in its proper place, after eight hours, is considered missing. This is even if it is used elsewhere in the building for experiments. Therefore, workers sign out all these types of materials taken to other areas of the building. If items are somehow removed from the building, and undetected after this time, it will appear to have been stolen. This is within one hour after business hours. This security is overseen by the powerful Captain Meyers, and his authority stretches across many lines.

All around the building, the May air is calm. Standing at any of its four sides, one could practically see forever. In the distance, there is so much land, hill and sky, and the nearby highway. It is only very busy when people from out-of-town come in to see friends, and relatives, who dwell here.

In the expanse of this area, there is an unsettling stillness. The only noise one can hear is the roar of planes speeding through the airways, and then fading slowly away. They seem muffled by clouds, as they pass over piercing the sky, like traveling into another world.

Birds fly by swiftly, and soon they soar high up into the air, performing dazzling displays of acrobats. There is water nearby too, and the sound of seagull's squawks come closer and closer. They swoop down searching for a perch, for a momentary rest.

When the afternoon grows late into nightfall, in this scientific part of the world, the scenery changes, and it becomes quite ominous. An engulfing-blue sky becomes streaked with soft clouds, in shades of pink and gray. A beautiful-setting sun casts a soft, shimmering, amber and gold-veiled hue upon homes and trees. Long shadows stretch upon paved streets and along hillsides, and blanket the ground. The remaining birds fly off into the horizon, and appear like tiny-black arches following the setting sun.

During the day, inside the laboratory building are two scientists, Paul DeAngelo and Theodore Cecil Clarke. They work in one of the laboratories on the seventh floor. They are working on individual computers that will assist each other in the process of cloning. Paul is a gorgeous man with shoulder length, curly-dark brown hair. It tumbles about him, as if it has a life of its own. Well over six-feet tall, with a dark-olive complexion, he seems almost too delicate to touch. He's charming, and carries himself with a heroic stature. He has a strong and sensual-authoritative voice that seems a bit intimidating. He is New American, which is a combination of African, Israeli and American. This wonderful mixture has created his good looks.

Theodore is somewhat attractive, a little odd, and on the slender side. Called TC for short, he has an unusually lanky frame. He has long legs and long arms, on a body that seems to lean forward as he walks. In some respects, he looks a little like a mad scientist. His huge glasses conceal his true-gentle identity. TC is a little wry, but very likable. He has a huge-hypnotic smile that has an amazingly warm effect on everyone.

They are both dressed in seamless-red jumpsuits, covered by white-laboratory coats. In opposite corners, at the back of their laboratory, are two-large closets for each scientist. There is a tiny changing, and seating area. There is also a seven-foot long, steel-assembly table at the center of the laboratory that both scientists share to do their work. It is so highly polished that is resembles glass.

45

Paul's cabinet is crammed with obsolete test tubes, dyes, syringes, and litmus paper. There are various-experimental materials and printouts, and their end results.

On one of Paul's shelves is a compound. It is in a large, five-inch wide and one-inch thick, transparent-steel glass jar. It is covered with a heavy-iron lid. Unknown to Paul, Jim Harrison has secretly incorporated Element G into this compound. It also went into the making of some of his computer-component devices that will be placed into his working computer.

The scientists have not yet met Jim, or the captain; as there is an enormous amount of secrecy when it comes to those in power. They are, however, aware that the captain has tremendous clout and oversees everything. Along with his power, his secrecy makes him a strange and illusive individual.

There are also shelves upon shelves of new and sophisticated equipment, materials, and chemical compounds supplied by DUG. The staff members, who assist the scientists, are in charge of the inventory kept in their closets. The scientists are unaware of the new materials that are placed in their closets. They only become aware, when a particular experiment is going to be performed that call for these materials.

Inside the left-side pocket of Paul's coat, are a couple of laser pens and scraps of foil papers, with their triangular-edges sticking out. In his left-breast pocket is a small, four-inch-transparent steel-glass tube. It has a black cap with a cork-type stopper, containing experimental material. Paul placed it in his pocket, as he did not want it on the table, with other experimental materials. The solution consists of a variety of DNA, beta data, computer-engineered beta receptors, and enhanced microorganisms. It also contains other organic materials in a chemical-compound mixture. It is to be used in the final phase of the computer assemblage. Unbeknownst to him, it also contains Element G. There is a transparent label adhered around the tube, with an undecipherable white-raised disk code. This code specifies the contents and usage of the tube, and for its protection. There is small-black lettering above the code that read, Dangerous Experimental Material Section #7E.

Opposite Paul's closet is a closet for TC, and it's full of microfiber-optical tubes. There is an array of computer equipment, computer parts, chemicals, and printouts. He also has shelves of sophisticated materials that in time will be of some use.

They work, talk and exchange-information steadily for hours. In the process, preparing chemicals, components and

47

parts, and genetic material needed for their cloning computers. They work from a blueprint, containing assembly directions that include all the materials needed.

Meanwhile, from the only window in their laboratory, the sun begins to radiate a glow that lights the room. Soon it will be time for the scientists to go home. Many of the components are spread out on the steel table, such as large computer sections, as well as various-colored smaller pieces. The largest parts look like a black, and hollowed-out ostrich egg, separated into a few sections. The front section is in four pieces, and the two-top halves have curved notches, near the bottom that resemble large and protruding-hooded eyelids. The two-bottom halves have two-curved notches at the top that join the two-top halves forming two eye sockets. The back portion is one solid piece that connects to all of the individual-front pieces.

It won't be much longer before it is assembled, and it will resemble a large-black egg with two-round eye sockets. The designs of the eyes resemble thick, pink-frosted bifocal lenses, fitted perfectly into each socket. There is a mesh-grid covering on each eye for protection, and refraction of light. This allows the light to have full-brilliant radiance, and is reminiscent of a lighthouse, and similar in concept.

At the center of each eye are dark openings, which are the mechanical pupils. Basically, it's an oval-computer face upon a pedestal, with two-pink eyes in the center. It is visually frightening to say the least. It is here, within the components of the computer's eyes, where Jim has incorporated most of Element G.

Next to the computer parts, and gently levitating across the table, are clear sheets of data. They are constantly changing shape and color, and moving about on their own. These sheets have charts with symbols, diagrams, and names. There are configurations, and an advanced-number system. Small, but intensely-powerful batteries are on the table, alongside many multi-colored tiny parts.

There are other unusual materials that are assembled onto a lightweight, transparent-metal sheet. The sheet has various-gold dots, and symbols, unrecognizable lettering and light swirls. Tiny gold cables are intertwined that resemble beautifully-braided strands of hair, lay crisscrossing one another. They will all be placed into the scientist's computers.

In other parts of the building, workers are dressed in regulated uniforms. They are in a hurry scurrying through long corridors, and going in and out of different rooms, and nearly having a collision or two. All of the workers are too tied into their work to even chat with co-workers about their daily lives.

Each worker, on every floor, has color-coordinated uniforms to match their section. The different colors correspond with the project. These uniforms are sophisticated jumpsuits, designed specifically, to protect the bodies they hold from various elements. This includes chemical spills, abrasions, and light energy. It also provides protection from sharp objects and radiation. They can detect changes in air quality, body temperature and rhythms, and various life-altering situations. It also tells the employer the worker's-health status, what has been consumed, and any prior exposure to anything before putting on their uniform.

It is not just worker protection, but more of a matter of an invasion of an individual's privacy, which allows the employer protection. This policy ensures direct access to an individual's personal history, intimate encounters, and any illegal-substances present. It enforces complete loyalty to the employer, and a worker is deemed one-hundred percent reliable.

Paul and TC are in the red-dress code, which is the highest-ranking color in the ROY G. BIV Color Scheme. The colors of the other sections follow: orange, yellow, and so forth. Members of their staff are dressed in a very-pale red.

The six-floors below continue the scheme: violet, of course, is of the lowest, but not least important. The eighth floor does not follow this scheme, as it is used for equipment storage.

On the seventh floor, where Paul and TC are working is called Section #7E. This section is not as lively as the other floors. It is very secluded, and it is where one of the most highly-kept, secretive-scientific projects is located. Floors five and six are the yellow and orange-color coordinated floors. They are assisting with cell samples for cloning, and computer data and parts.

Each floor has its own-individual job to do, by assisting scientists. Each working part, of any object created in the laboratory for experiments, requires assistance from each floor. Therefore, only one project or experiment can be worked on at a time, throughout the entire laboratory. Only upon completion, can another project begin. Although a joint effort, other floors are not allowed any knowledge of the final concept, which they are contributing. This ensures complete secrecy, and only those authorized will know the final outcome.

The other floors bring the rolling-metal tables of parts, and experimental materials into Section #7E for the scientists, and leave thereafter. Another staff worker will come back later, and bring out the table with any leftover materials. Most of the time, an empty table is brought back. They know not to gawk for any period of time, but just do what they must, and exit as quickly as possible.

The workers know that they are monitored on every floor, every moment, and on every angle. All projects created within this building are all classified as Universally-Secret Projects. Anyone who talks about it to someone else, within or outside of the building, can be silenced. If one were foolish enough to even make idle conversation, it would be certain someone of higher authority would quickly find out.

There are Infrascreens that are made into the walls, floors and ceilings throughout the building, which is barely detectable to the naked eye. It is an intricately-woven honeycomb mesh made into the cream-colored surroundings. The mesh is incredibly fine and flat, and would need an amplifying grid, or magnifying slide to see it up close. The room color appears ordinary, but the mesh serves as an optical network of nerves. It connects to an outer computer, monitored by other authorities.

In addition to the mesh, the floors are covered over with a thin and fibrous-acrylic surface that cannot be washed, or polished away. When someone or something comes into the room, and makes contact with the floor, or near a wall, it creates energy and static electricity. This is picked up through the mesh coverings. An electromagnetic field is also created in the room that is sent to a monitor, along with the optical network of information, for technical enhancement. This turns into crystal-clear images instantaneously. Nothing can escape it, and this is all done daily.

On this beautiful Thursday afternoon, Paul is leaving work early at 4:00 p.m. to catch up on a few errands, and on some things he needs to do at home. He walks towards his closet in the laboratory, and opens the door pulling out a duffle bag. He unzips it to reveal a rolled-up-gray sports jacket off to the left, and a pair of folded-casual jeans that look ready to be changed into. There are also a few folded T-shirts squeezed in the middle, next to a maroon-colored towel. As he digs through to the bottom of the bag, stuffed on the right, underneath all of this is a belt, and athletic footwear. He places on top of the bag, a half-empty glass bottle of a pale-red leftover health beverage. It looks warm and old, and has separated into various textures with brown-particles floating throughout.

As Paul digs, he glances back over his shoulder towards TC. He jokingly asks: "You did remember that I was leaving early today, didn't you?" As TC responds to him, the tube of solution falls out from his white-coat pocket, and into his bag out of view. Neither of them is aware of this. Paul walks to his little-private niche, and to a small bench out of view. He hastily changes into his jeans, T-shirt and sports jacket. Then, he sticks his UIS card in the front pocket of his jeans. He puts his laboratory clothing into his closet, and reaches for his bag. He zips it close, and throws the straps over his right shoulder and says, "Well guy, I'll see you tomorrow." TC smiles and replies sarcastically: "Sure! I guess I'll see you in here very early tomorrow, since you're getting an early start, huh?" Paul grins mischievously, and heads out the door.

He leaves and heads to a red elevator, then goes down to the main floor. There is a long corridor, which leads to a heavy-exit door, to the underground-parking garage. This is where he gets his solar-powered vehicle. On the outside of the building, Mannie the real guard has already begun its patrol.

It will take Paul about 10 to 12 minutes to reach home, as he drives at his usual neck-breaking pace to get there. Once he reaches home, he unlocks the door with a swift slide of his hand against the door's small-side panel.

His one level, buff-colored home is nearly empty except for a few furnishings, and the necessities he needs to get by. The buff décor seems almost unsuited for his outgoing personality. It looks almost clinical. He walks through the living room to his bedroom, and throws his duffle bag onto the bed. There is a soft clanking sound, like two pieces of glass hitting against each other. He opens the bag and muddles through, and to his astonishment, finds the tube containing the solution. Surprised by how it could have gotten into his bag without his notice, he decides to take the solution back to the laboratory before the building closes at 6:00 p.m.

He puts the tube into the left pocket of his gray-sports jacket, and rushes back out to his vehicle. He speeds back to the building to return the solution. Unknown to Paul, the cap on the tube has loosened. It is leaking, and seeping through to the front of his pocket.

Driving back through town on his way to the building, Paul rolls down the window. As he does, a soft-gentle breeze begins to blow. His silky-soft hair tumbles in the breeze, and shines with a sun-drenched radiance. He looks out through the windshield to take in a glorious, late-afternoon sky. While looking skyward, he notices something to the left, in the distance. It is a small-gray spot, sailing along very slowly. As he continues looking skyward, the laboratory building comes into view. It is also, off in the distance, but to the right. As he gets closer to the building, he starts to wonder if anyone else on the road or near the building sees what he's observing.

Neither the guard, nor anyone else is paying any attention to the sky. Paul, being of a scientific mind, slows down then stops, and continues to observe this strange spot. He notices that the spot actually appears to be an opening, like a ripped piece of fabric snagged on a nail. Also, being skeptical, he cannot bring himself to think that this could be some type of unexplained phenomenon.

The gray spot alters its course, and begins to move to the right. It now appears that the spot is actually the sky, as if torn open revealing deep darkness. Suddenly, he can see a gray object emerging from the darkness. In an instant, it is right in front of his vehicle. It is elongated and semi-transparent, as if made from mercury. There are no markings or mechanisms of any kind, as if a being all of its own.

Paul is stunned, as he continues to watch the object hover for a few seconds. It appears interdimensional, and can change sizes and distance. Suddenly, the object dashes away and hovers silently over the laboratory building. It flashes an enormously, bright-white light three times, as though communicating. Paul is absorbed and awestruck at the same time. He thinks he is seeing a real, unidentified-flying object, and gets out of his vehicle to get a better look. He jokingly says aloud: "This is like those stories on Screenview. Someone gets out of their vehicle, and they're abducted. I don't believe this!"

As he leaves his vehicle, he somehow feels a kinship of some kind that he cannot explain. It is, as though, a strange connection has taken place. It seems to him that the object is an intelligent-spiritual being, as opposed to a vehicle being guided by intelligence. As he slowly walks towards the building and towards the object, there is another small flash like that of an old-Polaroid camera. The object dashes towards the opening in the sky, and disappears. Before he realizes it, he is back in his vehicle again, and there is nothing above him. He looks at his watch to see if he lost time, like many others have reported, but no time has passed since he first saw the object. It is actually five minutes earlier than it should be. He decides to wait awhile in his vehicle, until he can figure out what has just happened. He sits on the driver's side of his vehicle with the door open. His legs hang out, while his feet nervously tap upon the road. He has second thoughts now as to all of the abduction stories that he did not believe. He waits for a few more moments before continuing, very slowly, to the laboratory.

Strangely, the highway is completely empty. His heart is pounding nearly through his chest. He places his hand over his jacket's breast pocket, as though trying to quell it. When he pulls his hand away, he notices there is something shining on it. There is also a dark spot on his pocket. He reaches in and removes the tube. The cap has risen up, and the solution has spilled over the sides. He reaches into his vehicle's compartment, and pulls out a long-white handkerchief. He wipes his hand and the sides of the tube, and then places both the handkerchief, and tube back into the same pocket. His hand and the spot on his pocket begin to glimmer. He then feels a warm sensation against his chest area, and is not sure what to make of it. He looks out through the windshield, and towards the sky, again. He is beginning to believe that there is some intelligence involved, and this intelligence may have some sort of connection to the building.

Suddenly, he feels a strange and sharp sensation in the middle of his forehead that comes on quickly. He slams on the brakes, and grabs his forehead, while the other hand holds the steering wheel. He feels a strange, raised area on his forehead, and gropes at it with his fingers. He becomes alarmed, and does not know what's happening to him. His forehead appears as if, there has been a small-square implantation of some sort, placed underneath the skin. As he fingers it more closely, he gasps aloud: "This thing feels like a computer part or something. What is this?" For a moment or so, he feels very strange: incredibly sleepy, disoriented and controlled, but the feeling quickly passes.

As he resumes driving, he is inclined to look in the rear-view mirror for oncoming traffic. For some reason, has knowledge that nothing is approaching. He looks for traffic on either side, and his expression is that of perplexity. It seems there hasn't been any traffic for quite some time. It is as though, he is caught in a suspended moment in time.

Looking up at the sky once again, he notices that the object is there, directly above the building. The object flashes a few times, and completely disappears into the ripped opening in the sky. The sky closes quickly, and all appears normal. Once arriving at the building, he parks at the curb. He passes Mannie, and goes through the heavy doors to the laboratory to where TC is still working. He pretends that he left something in his closet. Being in constant view, he does not get an opportunity to remove the tube from his pocket.

He could forget the whole matter, if it wasn't for the fact of security, and the monitoring of materials once they are removed. With much concern on his face TC asks: "Hey man, are you alright? You look like you've seen a ghost or something. Are you all right? Is that why you came back, or did you forget something? What did you forget?" Paul tries to regain his composure, and then turns to him and says: "Yeah, sure! I left my UIS card here somewhere. It must have fallen out when I opened my duffle bag."

As he opens his closet, pretending to look around for it, his curly-brown hair whips his forehead. TC does not let him out of his sight, and Paul is still unable to remove the tube from his pocket. TC says, "You've got something on your jacket!" Paul's heart is pounding, as a rush of adrenaline surges though his body like electricity. His skin tingles, and he becomes flush, and thinks of a quick lie. He says: "I drank some of the drink in my bag when I was driving, and I must have spilled it. Thanks! I'll clean it when I reach home."

TC stares at him oddly and wonders what Paul is hiding. Paul fumbles through his jean-pant pockets, and the card falls to the floor. TC says: "I think you're losing it man. You've got your card in your pocket all along, and you come all the way back here to look for it." Again, he stares strangely at Paul, with a look of suspicion and mistrust. Paul just stands awkwardly, not knowing what to say or do. He then replies: "I couldn't find it when I got home." He fumbles his hands around, uncomfortably, in his pockets trying his best to look innocent of the situation.

It is now time for TC to go home, and as he prepares to leave, Paul leaves before him. As Paul pushes opens the heavy-exit door leading out of the building, he carelessly bumps against it. More of the solution rises up, and spills out into his jacket pocket. Once outside, he panics, and looks around to see if anyone is watching. He's anxious and fumbling trying to rid the leaking tube without being seen. He pulls out the white handkerchief, and wraps it around the tube. He quickly throws it into the surrounding-hedge grown fence. It hits the dirt, and lodges under a portion of the jagged edge. The handkerchief lies on the soil with a corner of it being lifted up and down by a soft-gentle breeze.

Paul momentarily stands hunched over it, as though waiting for something to happen to the solution. At that moment, the door swings opens behind him, and he straightens up, and looks back startled. He fixes his attire, and quickly gets control of himself. Exiting from the door is TC. Again, Paul looks as though he has seen a ghost, but retains his composure. This time TC is really suspicious, and worried. He is thinking, "Why hasn't he left?"

TC is getting a lift today because of vehicle trouble, and he is leaving his vehicle parked in the underground garage. He finds it peculiar that Paul didn't head straight back to his vehicle, and just go home. He asks directly: "Do you need a ride or something?" Paul just stands sheepishly by the building, as though waiting for someone. He folds his arms across his chest to seem relaxed, and to hide his stained-jacket pocket. He answers: "No, I'm just waiting for someone, I'm okay. Thanks!" He waits patiently for TC to leave, glancing at his watch display and smiles.

TC heads towards his ride but shouts back: "You're acting strange man. I hope whoever you're waiting for isn't from outer space, a space cadet," he says jokingly walking away, and disappears out of sight.

As Paul continues standing outside of the building with his arms folded across his chest, something suddenly catches his eye. It is Mannie who notices him, as he pretends to be waiting for someone to approach, from the far side of the building. Paul is anxious, and keeps checking his solar-wrist watch. Then he paces around the corner of the building, until he is out of view.

Suddenly, Mannie glimpses the handkerchief on the ground under the fence. The wind has blown the handkerchief and it looks like white trash, and the tube can be slightly seen. Slowly walking towards it, while bending down, it looks around to see if anyone is watching. Mannie slides its left hand under the fence's sharp edge, and finds it cannot fit. While pushing back a little dirt to see what the object may be, it again looks around to see if anyone notices. Manny opens part of the handkerchief with its fingertips, and discovers the tube nearly pulling it through.

There are footsteps heard coming from behind, and Mannie quickly withdraws its hand. In doing so, causes the remaining solution to spill out across its hand, while simultaneously cutting it on the sharp edge of the fence. This combination causes it quite a bit of pain. The footsteps draw closer as Mannie now smiling and nodding, gains its composure. A worker heading for home comes into view. As a fusion, it has to be careful as workers can report him for suspicious actions.

Mannie examines its hand, and notices that the pain and the cut are mysteriously gone. Perplexed, it does not discuss this with anyone, but goes about patrolling, as if nothing has happened.

Meanwhile, Paul comes back around from the side of the building. He sees Mannie standing in the same spot looking strange. He suspects it must know something, and decides to forget the whole matter. Uneasy about his earlier experience in his vehicle, he's not sure whether to drive, or walk down the long-hilly path to the terminal for a ride. There he can get a solar vehicle or several of the new, around-the-clock solar and propulsion-shuttle vehicles. He decides to drive his own vehicle.

When Paul arrives home, he is disheveled and intensely worried, and wondering whether to go back to the laboratory. He closes the door, swipes it, and locks it securely with his hand. He braces his back against the door, as though someone or something had been following him. He stands this way for several moments, with his tilted head, resting against the door. He begins thinking that he has put something grisly in motion, and its outcome has yet to come to light. He straightens himself up, and walks hastily into the bedroom. He removes his jacket and throws it onto the bed. It slides off and hits the floor, and he notices the soiled spot where the solution has spilled. He walks towards the jacket and picks it up. For a moment, he thinks he sees something moving. It looks like floaters that people get when they bend down, and get up too quickly. He dismisses it at first. When he looks at the jacket again, he sees tiny-little spots moving around in a circular motion, which quickly dissipates in front of his eyes. He throws it onto a cushioned chair in the corner of the room, and plops down frightened onto the bed. He sits on the edge of his bed with his heart racing, and obsessively thinks of going back to the laboratory. Then suddenly, he feels a warm-moving sensation coming out his right nostril. He touches it, and realizes he's having a nosebleed. He jumps from the bed, and rushes into the bathroom and looks into the mirror. Taking a piece of bathroom tissue to wipe his nose, he stares in the mirror a few moments observing it and his forehead. There are several-vertical welts on his forehead, and he begins to throw cold water on his face. While doing so, the blood dripping from his nose mixes with the water tunneling down the drain, turning into a pale-red mixture. Overwhelmed and stressed, he holds onto the sink, and leans over and bows his head in prayer. He takes a small-white towel and places it under his nose, and goes back into the bedroom. He walks slowly to the chair, again, peering over his jacket trying to make sense of all that has taken place. Sitting on the edge of the bed dumfounded, he slides back with the towel under his nose trying to stop his mind from racing. He keeps thinking about the monitored-displaced tube of solution with his fingerprints on it. In his mind, he hopes it won't get into the wrong hands, or by anyone in the building.

He removes the towel, and instead of seeing blood, he sees tiny-gray spots moving in a circular motion. He gives in to his fears, and what just might be happening to him. Rolling the towel, he quickly throws it onto the jacket. Holding his head, and lying back worrying, he wonders: "What if someone sees it? What if they pick it up? I've got to get the solution! I have to... oh, I... I have to go back to..." As though suddenly sedated, he rests his arms by his sides, and falls into an uncontrollable deep-deep sleep. Everything seems to slip away, and all seems forgotten.

CHAPTER 3

The next day Friday, May 30th, the workers at the laboratory and research building are still scurrying around as usual. Paul enters the building with trepidation. He looks around the fence area for traces of what had happened the day before. Everything seems normal, as if it never occurred. He proceeds to his section, and joins TC, but there is something missing about him today. Something he, himself, cannot put his finger on, nor does he convey. He's anxious and feeling weird, and unusual, and experiencing déjà vu. Also, he has a sense of something impending, something he can't quite comprehend. He is not like his usual self, which is usually poised, confident, and organized when going about his work. He is hapless, deep in thought and unfocused, as if part of him is still at home. He is in between two spaces of time at once. Physically, he is in the laboratory, but mentally, seeming to have never left home. Yet, both parts of him are aware of each other.

While periodically touching his forehead, he tries not to bring attention to himself. Unfortunately, TC asks: "Why do you keep grabbing your forehead? I've noticed you keep touching it, as though you want to make sure it's still there." Paul sheepishly replies: "Oh, I've got this headache that I woke up with. It's nothing." TC says jokingly: "Well, let me tell you, your head's still intact." Fortunately for Paul, TC does not take his actions too seriously. He is quite busy adding the finishing touches to his computer. It is as though, he is working through some invisible timeline that only he is aware. Both continue to work throughout the day, putting together the small components that will make up two-complete working computers that will become cloning computers.

Paul constantly looks at the solar-powered-time display on the wall, as the afternoon-sun splashes golden light throughout the room. Once they have finished for the day, they will put their work on the table, and change clothing as usual. They both look at each other with a sigh of relief, as though they have performed some strenuous-physical task that has left them drained. As they prepare to leave, Paul seems to be in a trance. He is unable to shake the uncomfortable feelings he has been experiencing. They exit the laboratory, and TC pats him on the back and says: "Get some rest Paul, and have a good weekend."

On Saturday, May 31st at 9:30 a.m., Paul is at home getting ready to go out. Again, he doesn't feel much like himself. He doesn't feel the way he did at the laboratory, but something is still not quite right. Already feeling restless, he hurries into the shower, comes out and gets dressed in a huff. While looking in the mirror, he zips up his pants, and adjusts his belt. He has nagging thoughts of what happened at the laboratory.

As he rushes out of the house to his vehicle, he eats at a nearby café and reads from a Screenview. He uses his pale red, ultimate-identification system card, also known as a UIS Card, for his meal, and all of his purchases and resources. It is an incredible-card system that makes him part of the Universal-Identification System. It is the only one-of-its kind with multiple functions: identification, financial information, debits and credit features. It is also used for health care benefits. Initially, to receive all of these benefits, all of an individual's personal information is taken. Such information includes a full-body photograph, blood type, DNA, date of birth and the like. Then, the individual's background information is gathered such as place of birth, residences and employment. There is no photograph of the cardholder on the card, as this information is already stored in the system, and appearance can easily be change if someone has cosmetic alterations done.

The first piece of information taken, when the card is used, is the cardholder's identity. Then their face and aura are taken next. Their health status and other information will be taken, if necessary, depending upon the situation, which will match the same information that was initially placed into the system. Name and address are important as well, and residences, but only on an as needed bases. This information is automatically updated regularly. This card issuance needs only to be done once, and begins upon the user's birth. The UIS Card is sensed through sensitive systems that displays on monitors, and Screenviews out of the cardholders view. Throughout the individual's life, their information will continuously change. These changes include health status, and marital status. It also includes going to the doctor or hospital, and traveling.

As the ultimate card, it uses the ultimate-tracking system for updating any and all information that the individual cardholder will encounter. Once they present the card, their health information is extracted and updated. All information is sent to the universal system, and there is nothing for the cardholder to do. Unfortunately, the drawback for the cardholder is that he or she is helpless without it.

Along the bottom of the pale-red card are ridges, which contain codes representing the actual fingerprints of each finger of the user. The complete-outer surface of the card has a special surface that retains the user's fingerprints for up to 90 minutes after use. This special surface also retains an individual's aura field. This ultimate protection has eliminated the fear of a card being stolen. Also, when the fingertips of the user come into contact with the surface of the card, the card

70

contacts the universal system, and it can instantly identify the cardholder. When used at establishments, unauthorized purchases cannot be done on a lost or if stolen card.

The card system also corresponds to the individual's voice, which is matched with a series of numbers and letters that connect to a system, located at all establishments. There is one last feature for safeguarding the card against tampering, or if lost or stolen for any reason. It actually turns black after 30 minutes, if the cardholder's aura field is no longer detectable within a certain distance. It becomes deactivated if handled by someone else, unless returned to the user immediately. Another card can be issued if lost or damaged to the cardholder at any authorized establishment. All vital information is permanently stored so there is no room for error. If the cardholder has a twin, it is possible that the aura fields may be indistinguishable, but the stored information differentiates siblings.

While Paul is reading in the café, he sips on a steaming-hot cup of coffee, and nibbles on a BLT sandwich. He's trying to take his mind off of the laboratory, but the restless feeling continues to come over him.

Finishing his sandwich and coffee, he uses his UIS card towards payment, and for the tip. He gets up hesitantly, and leaves the café. He drives around to clear his mind, but nothing quells his anxiety. Once he returns home, he sits on the sofa, and ponders his next move. He's much too restless, and cannot stay still and heads to the bedroom. After a quick look in the mirror, he heads out the door again. He is anxious, and wants to get back to the building, and thinks it may be best to rent a vehicle. Also, if anyone were there, they wouldn't recognize him, but he reconsiders the idea.

While driving in his vehicle on this quiet-Saturday morning, he anxiously cruises along. Along the route towards the building, the sky is beautiful, clear and bright. The clouds appear soft and fluffy like cotton, and are scattered across an endless sky. Strangely, they seem to stay in the same position for some time. He looks out through the windshield, observing the clouds, and daydreaming of a time when he was younger. He imagines the clouds taking on shapes of faces, animals, and even places. He is nearly in a trance, while trying to keep his eyes on the road. The clouds seem to hypnotize him into an almost-melancholy daydream.

Approaching a turn, there are many tall and narrow trees that lead into a large-open field. He has to pass this area before he gets to the laboratory. Once leaving this area, he glimpses something above-treetop level in front of him, traveling quite fast. It appears like a gray spot moving amongst the clouds.

Paul begins to feel that strange pain in his forehead again, and déjà vu. It is the same-strange object, and it is heading straight for the laboratory. He speeds up to keep up with the object, but it's much faster, and disappears behind the building.

Once arriving at the building, he gets out of his vehicle, and looks skyward. He wonders where the object may have disappeared. He decides to search the area, as there seems to be no one around. As he nears the fence where he dropped the tube of solution, he is disrupted and shocked to see someone on the right side of the building. Paul says aloud, "That's strange!" Thinking that he is seeing things he says: "There is no building patrol on weekends." Being quite surprised, he mumbles to himself, "Is that Mannie?" It is and it heads for Paul, and the fence area where it tried to retrieve the tube. It appears in an altered state, and doesn't seem to see him.

Paul peers around the area, and cannot believe his eyes. The area is overgrown with hedge, as an out-of-control growth spurt has taken place.

When Mannie approaches Paul, he notices its left hand. There is a strange skin transformation on the top, where it sustained the cut from the fence. The skin appears mutated, and is very much discolored. It looks hardened, and painful to the touch. As Paul looks on, there seems to be something happening to Mannie physically. It has a fixed gaze upon its face, and its entire body becomes surrounded by a faint-white haze. Paul stares and steps back in horror, as it becomes a wraith, disappearing into another existence, and dimension.

At that very moment, eerily above them, appears the same-gray object that had been traveling at a very-high speed. It hovers silently, as though it is waiting for something. Paul is terrified, but he cannot move. Nor can he take his eyes off of the object, or Mannie. In an act of desperation, he manages to gather up enough strength, and runs to his vehicle. He doesn't look back, but jumps in and slams the door, and speeds away.

The object then ascends over Mannie, who is nearly transparent, as its body begins to flicker in and out of existence. For a brief moment, it seems translucent, then becomes solid and then, transparent again. Then it is gone. The object-above flashes brightly, and shoots up and across the sky with an incredible brilliance.

As Paul drives home, he can see the object streak across the sky. It, again, flashes very brightly, three times, as if communicating. It continues outward and upwards disappearing into an opening in the afternoon sky. Paul truly believes now that he's had an incredible experience, and is at a loss as to what to do. He is realizing in his mind, this object must be claiming Mannie for the solution.

He arrives at home, and wants to forget about what has just happened, but is unable to shake the terrible feelings of the experience. Being of a sound-scientific mind, he doesn't think much of strange happenings. He always tries to find a rational explanation for almost anything, and if not, he tries to ignore it. This he cannot ignore, and he thinks to himself: "I wonder if I should mention this to anyone?"

He is shaking terribly and decides to reach out to someone, and chooses TC. He sends a thought and verbal message that is picked up through a sensitive-wafer implant inside his ear. He sits patiently in his living room for an answer. As he does, he suddenly begins to feel extremely fatigued, as though the last terrifying moments has suddenly caught up with him. His forehead begins to throb like a sinus headache, and he places his hand up against it. As he heads for the bedroom, his foot hits the leg of the bed, and he trips. He stumbles, and lies down for what he feels will be just a quick nap. Paul finds he's going into a deep-uncontrollable sleep.

Paul sleeps for many hours, and awakens in a bad state on Sunday. He spends the afternoon at home, trying to piece together the last 24-hours of what has happened to him. Still being very-much disoriented, he tries to eat a little food to quell his nerves, and to stop him from thinking. Nibbling on crackers and preparing to make soup is when he realizes, he hasn't eaten for some time. Strangely, he is not really hungry.

He sits down in the kitchen baffled, and unable to communicate with anyone to explain what has occurred. He turns off the heat plate and covers the soup; leaving the crackers on the table, he goes into the living room.

While activating the Screenview, he glances over the news without really concentrating on anything particular. His Screenview covers an area in the middle of his living room, from the ceiling, to nearly touching the floor. It works with invisible-energized vibrating particles that receive messages, and images sent through the air and through a HSD.

The various sports selections, also, cannot hold his attention. He is pondering in his mind, why the last couple of days seem just like minutes. His memory is becoming elusive, and it is becoming, increasingly, difficult to remember certain things and events. He stops watching the programs, and begins to pace around the room.

He sits down, stands up and checks the solar-time wall display, then sits again. Lying across the couch does not calm him. He cannot concentrate on Screenview either, and switches from program to program. Rushing through the bedroom, he enters the bathroom. He looks into the mirror and stares at his forehead, as though the answer will come. Leaving the bathroom, he sits on the right corner of the foot of his bed. He lies back staring at the ceiling, playing over and over the events in his head, and suddenly drift off to sleep.

While asleep, the table-top-solar time display alarm goes off, suddenly awakening him. He sits up on the bed and for a moment, disoriented, shuts off the alarm. It reads Monday, June 1st, 7:08 a.m. "Monday?" Paul says astonished. "Monday?" He says again. Then he laments, "I just went to sleep!"

He unwittingly prepares himself for work, and hurries to his vehicle. He is ready very early today, which is unusual for him. Upon reaching the laboratory building, he sees a shadowy glimpse of something on the far-right side above the hedges. Paul is thinking: "Maybe it is a scientist or another

77

security guard, or maybe just my lack of sleep." It is a very eerie, black-shapeless form, which moves in a gliding and stop motion. It travels like smoke, and begins to ascend upward to the seventh floor to Section #7E. It then appears like a hole on the side of the building, and it disappears like a ghost near the closed window.

Paul mumbles from his vehicle: "That is definitely not a man, security, or for that matter human." Before he reaches the building, that same strange-gray object appears in the sky, just above the laboratory. The black-shapeless form appears, again, now existing from a black void in the window. It then goes to the top of the building, and towards the oval object. It dissipates into the object, and both speed off into the morning sky.

Paul has a strange revelation in his mind: "That black shape must be Mannie, and it must be dead. Maybe while alive it mixed with the solution, and the spirit was transformed. It must have remained, and had to be taken away for some reason. I wonder why it went to the window." He then gets an unsettling feeling and says aloud: "It must have been looking for me or the solution!" Now he is starting to believe, he has a larger role to play in future events and happenings.

Those who work in the building, arrive in their vehicles making quick turns to enter the parking garage, as other vehicles whiz by. Paul parks there as well, and goes to his section and does not mention anything to anyone. To his amazement, TC doesn't seem to know or sense anything.

The scientists greet each other, and TC is in a good mood. Paul gives him a fake almost mischievously smile. He is not sure if TC is aware of what he is concealing. Normally, when they are together, they make each other act childlike. They become filled with excitement, and act like two boys who are at a ball game, when they are supposed to be at school. Similar is their thrill, when they are working on a secret project.

As they work together on finishing their computers, no one in the building is aware of the strange events occurring that morning. Only Paul knows that someone or something has entered their laboratory.

There are tell-tale signs their computers were tampered with. Some parts that have been assembled have become disassembled, and there's a strange air within their laboratory.

They simultaneously sense something is a little off, but they stare off in the distance dumbfounded. Then they stare at each other briefly, but neither says a word. Although not watching each other while working, they both have looks of suspicion on their faces. Soon their thoughts are cleared away, and they begin to converse with each other. Basically, the computers are complete; the scientists are just applying the finishing touches.

Paul's computer will be called Project Eyesic, pronounced I-sick. It will be operated simply by placing a solar powered, and energized-maze cartridge into its' side panel. It has two-round-projector eyes also known as screens at the front of it. The mechanical eyes are designed to administer rays of infrared light, and bright pink to deep-pink energy light. It does not look like any other computer or machine that has been made before. It is a large, jet-black-oval mechanical ball, sitting on a long-black tubular stand. The large-piercing eyes are protected by frosted, off-white-transparent steel caps of mesh in a crisscross pattern. Above the eyes are semi-cylindrical black lids that protrude outwards. They are reminiscent of street-traffic lights. These lights are no longer in use, but were hung high directly over roadways to direct traffic, and assist people crossing the street. They housed lighting in red, yellow and green that was attached in a row horizontally and vertically. They can now only be found in museums.

The inner parts of Eyesic eyes are like those of Screenview, and based on the same concept. Its eyes also called its screens are wired to the back of solid screens, inside the oval enclosure. The oval head of quartered halves are now completely assembled, and done with such seamless accuracy, that it actually looks whole. It is completely smooth to the touch, and looks cold, and eerie and almost living. There is a closed slit on its side, where a cartridge is placed, with stored-cloning information for programming.

The cartridge is a three-inch-square block and about one quarter of an inch thick. It contains several HSD's, which are separated by magnets that keep them from touching, as well as prevent them from going in the same direction. There are also power cells in this cartridge, as well as in Eyesic, which can generate quite-a-bit of power. It is quite a sight to behold, and scary to say the least. Eyesic seems sinister even when not functioning, and it takes on a human-like quality.

TC has a completely different type of computer. His is a small, flat, rotating-metal table with a highly-reflecting surface called a Skid. Placed several inches above it, on a thin column, is a large MCR. It has a base below it for recording data, and replicating cloning information that is placed into it. It doesn't look much like a computer at all. In fact, it looks so simplistic that it seems, it couldn't do any more than a hand-held mirror, but this is refined technology. It is called RFactor. There are circuits, and controls off to the side for operation, but only a trained individual can operate it. It still looks as though it is in the development stage, even though it is complete. Both will be used together for experiments.

Unlike Eyesic, RFactor is not programmable, and TC or a trained individual will need to operate it. The MCR will contain all of the information for cloning that it extracts from the materials placed on the Skid, and vice versa. RFactor's MCR has the capability to capture cloning material, and replicate everything about it on a small scale upon the skid. Whether that be structurally, or genetically, and replicate it to perfection. It replicates to actual size creating a structural base for Eyesic to work from.

The genetic information captured in the MCR reflects upon the Skid. It is Eyesics job to clone the information onto another surface. It could be on a wall, door or just into existence. If a person were to make contact with the Skid at the time of operation, it could extract and replicate their genetic makeup, and everything needed for replication.

RFactor's ability is to supply the information for Eyesic to bring the experiment further along. Precaution and expertise is required so that there are no chances for errors. It is hoped that these computers will become the ultimate-cloning vehicles.

Paul and TC's laboratory door swings open, and two serious-looking young men enter wearing pale-red jumpsuits. One is pushing a large, steel, two-tiered rolling table, while the other leans way over to hold the door for him. They have come to take the computers to an experimental laboratory within the building. Escorted by the scientists, the computers are mounted onto the table. They are wheeled down a long-white hall to an elevator that is enormous. It is wide and deep, and has a single, red-curved door that is eight-inches thick. It engulfs one as he or she approaches it. There are no buttons to push, but invisible heat and aura sensors that instruct the elevator which way to go. It knows where and which floor to go when picking up riders. A voice system can state where the elevator is located, and which floor or area the elevator is heading. On the inside, there are also several Screenviews showing various areas. One can visually indicate where they would like to go. An individual's voice is also acceptable, as the elevator seem to have a life of its' own.

When the elevator opens its single door, it opens strong and quickly. With the swiftness of its' opening, it is as though, it is inviting one to enter. There is an atmosphere within like its holding a secret, and one has to enter at-their-own risk to discover it. Once the door closes, it is isolated from the rest of the world. There is no window and no sound, but just swift movement, and it is over.

The two-young men and the scientists enter a huge and dimly-lit room. The walls and ceiling are metal with a rusty, burnt-sienna color treatment, and dull-gold lines streaked haphazardly throughout. The 60-foot long walls are 15-feet high, and practically stretch out right before one's eyes.

Upon entering the room, there is a single, very-bright red light source directly in front of them in the distance. It is dead center on the end wall close to the ceiling. It is self-sustaining, and intelligent.

Inside the room, the light from the hall behind them, allows them to see somewhat more into the room. On the right side of the room, protruding out the wall is a large, yellow-arched 3-D screen. On the left side of the room is a windowed enclosure. This is where the scientist will be protected while operating the computers, when the experiment is taking place. Also, along this perimeter near the scientists, is where the computers will be placed to perform the experiment. There are also unused computers, and computer parts strewn everywhere. There are boxes piled high in various places amongst vast, and strangely-shaped unrecognizable items.

The arched, 3-D screen is 20-feet long by 8-feet high and made into the wall, and it is seamless. It emits radiance like that of a huge-light box, and looks like artwork taken to the extreme. On the same wall, next to the screen on the right is a windowed area into a separate room. A technician can peer from this window into the area, and also see the scientists. It also allows the scientists to see the technician.

There are hundreds of horizontal shelves and sections compacted within the interior of the 3-D screen. It contains interconnecting-interfacing sections, and compartments for specific-cell material that will be sent to the 3-D screen by RFactor and Eyesic. One shelf will collect blood type and its entire make up and structure, as another collects genetic traits and DNA. The next section collects immune-system information of diseases that were acquired and treated, and diseases currently present in the body. This includes viruses, bacteria and any other foreign matter that may be residing within an individual. Illnesses that lie dormant are also detected and their antibodies are replicated for future cures and treatments. The remaining shelves have numerous other tasks to perform, which involves genetic-personality assessments, metaphysical, and natural abilities and an individual's evolution.

When human-beings cells are cloned in this way, all biological information will be perfectly separated, and can be replicated with an accuracy rate of one-hundred percent. Thus, by doing so, it is wiping out all diseased, viral and bacterial-infected cells without affecting healthy cells.

These replicated cells, and materials are then removed from these shelves to be placed back into the same individual, or someone else. If someone is receiving these cells, they are already lying at the back side of the screen on a platform.

The replicated cells are tagged, and are held on the shelves in individual-clear containers. They get pushed towards the back, as container-after-container is added, until the shelf is filled. Thereafter, they can be used, or they can just be stored. As the cells are quite small, this can continue over and over again, as the process does not take much time. They will be readily available for an individual, or individuals for cloning.

Behind the screen is a large and bare-adjoining room, with a flat-rectangular table that sits directly in the center called The Manifold. It is attached to the shelves by a network of micro-transparent fibers, traveling under the table through the floor that runs to the base of the screen. They travel back upwards through its four, polished, transparent-steel legs. The table is 10-feet in length, five-feet wide, and nine-inches thick. Its silvery appearance resembles dull-stainless steel. A closer inspection reveals that it is actually translucent.

Although the table appears hard, it is smooth and comfortable. Its core is a plastic-bubble mat, with individual and evenly-spaced cylindrical pores that extend to the bottom of the table. These pores are openings, and are about the size of a drinking-glass coaster, and each is connected to the underlying networks. The entire mat surface is made up of a material that has the duality of plastic, and metal with properties of both. Yet, it is flexible and strong. It also stays at a comfortable room temperature, and regulates accordingly. The Manifold is where the recipient lies during the experiment to receive cloned cells, and where materials are extracted from the participant.

One of the young men fishes around the room, and motions with his palm against a small and glowing, pale-blue protrusion on the wall. The room is now lit with a very low, diffused, energy-lighting source. It is also self-sustaining, as there are no light fixtures. The two men leave the table and computers in the room, and then exit. Two other men enter the room, wheeling another two-tiered experimental table, with folded-green sheets at the bottom. The top tier is carrying a New-American nude man lying quietly under a green sheet.

His name is Nade, and he is a very handsome study, but with a very virulent form of prostate cancer. These men also leave, but are scheduled to return in a few minutes to remove him, once the procedure is performed.

He is going to have some unhealthy-cancer cells, and healthy cells extracted. The cells will be sent to the shelves, where only the healthy cells will later be replicated indefinitely. This is after being treated with the blue dye, and energy to completely eradicate the cancer. Treated cells will be housed temporarily on certain shelves, and the cancerous portion that's destroyed will be on another to be analyzed.

The scientists enter their room in the laboratory. They look around the entire-huge space. It is as if, there is some sort of invisible source telling them of some hidden secrets within the walls. The distant red-light source casts a chilling glow on the objects in the room, summoning a foreboding atmosphere. It is like observing a nocturnal ceremony where there are dancers around a fire, and they are bathed in its glow. The glow also casts ominous shadows upon their surroundings. There is a spiritual feeling that abounds. The darkened and motionless-strange shapes of computer parts appear like ancient statues of centuries passed.

Entering the room, next to the 3-D screen from an unseen location, is a very inquisitive-looking man. He is the technician, Mr. Stewart. As he looks through the window to the scientists, it is with a permanent and quizzical expression on his face. He has large, bright, blue-gray eyes that penetrate through his glasses. He is wearing all white, but he has a red stripe across his left-breast pocket. He also wears a band of ROY G. BIV scheme on his sleeve revealing his areas of expertise.

Mr. Stewart then leaves his windowed area, and reenters through the doors the scientists initially came through. He approaches the computers, and puts a cartridge into Eyesic. He then returns back to his area, as the scientists look on.

From his room, using voice intelligence, Mr. Stewart instructs TC to power up RFactor, and to move it towards Nade, and position the MCR over his abdomen. After a few moments and with everything in place, the experiment begins. TC returns to the room. RFactor begins making clicking and sliding noises as the MCR moves into position, and begins extracting cells from him. The cells are taken quickly and placed upon the Skid.

Paul is then instructed to position Eyesic near RFactor's Skid to administer light energy from its eyes upon it. He then returns to the room with TC. Within the dimly-lit huge space, Eyesic eyes begin to illuminate. The pink light skims across the Skid's highly-reflective surface, reflecting these cells with light energy onto the 3D screen.

Suddenly, the laboratory door bursts open and quickly strutting in is the authoritative Captain Meyers with his own MCR. Two odd-looking men are with him rolling in twin babies on an experimental table. It is a boy and girl two-months old. It is a surprise to everyone in the room. Nade is pushed to the side by one of the captains men, and he quickly sits up startled with a look of concern on his face. He completely covers himself with the green sheet.

The captain then takes the cartridge from Eyesic, and replaces it with another. As its eyes quickly begin to turn a frightful-deep pink, it resembles an animal's eyes glowing in the dark. He then takes his MCR and scans it over the infants, and then passes it over the Skid.

Nade covers his eyes, as Eyesic blasts the light upon the Skid that reflects onto the screen. Frightfully, the infants are cloned in their entirety onto The Manifold. The captain removes the cartridge, and a devious and victorious smile comes upon his face.

Mr. Stewart and the scientists come out of their areas baffled, and shocked. Mr. Stewart shouts, "What is the meaning of this?" The captain gives him a frightful glare, and just stares at him, as if to silence him.

No one else in the room say a word. They know cloning cells isn't supposed to be done this way, and why and how could the captain have done this. TC and Paul look at each other completely puzzled, as the odd men stand silently.

The captain firmly commands both of the men with him: "Go in that room, and get the twins out of there!" They leave and go through Mr. Stewart's area, and enter the room with The Manifold retrieving the babies. They return, and place the twins upon the experimental table next to the original twins. The cloned babies appear exactly the same: identical-eye color, features, and medium-skin coloring.

He then instructs the two-odd men to remove all-four babies from the room. As he does, TC and Paul look into each cloned-child's eyes, and notice something strange in their appearance. Their skin has a translucency, as if the characteristics of real-skin cells were not duplicated. Something is missing and wrong. There is hollowness in their deeply-vacant expression. The scientists say nothing, but give each other a particularly-strange look.

The captain takes his cartridge from Eyesic, and turns to leave. He stops and says: "I just wanted to show you, there are alternative ways of permanently curing the sick. This illustration is the real power of cloning. This is just a test, and I will be performing others later. That is to say, tests, of what I am able to do. There are many things that I have discovered using the MCR, but for now, let's focus on the sick, and dying."

He goes on to say: "No further experiments will be conducted, until I say so. As you will see, I have many ideas about experimentation in the future; in time, it will be discovered." Then, he quickly leaves without saying anything further.

Those left in the room are mortified, and do not know what to do. They have become aware of his power, and believe this was a catastrophic demonstration. No one wants to ask any questions, as they are too afraid by what they've just witnessed. They do not have any authority or privacy; nor did they have advanced notice of this unsettling incident. The scientists have quickly become aware that future experiments can be dramatically altered. Also, they know that the medicinal purpose that this form of cloning is designed to serve, has been changed forever and they cannot say a word.

As Nade stare at the scientists, Mr. Stewart walks towards the table and places the original cartridge back into Eyesic. As soon as he does, Eyesic begins to make strange noises, and is believed to be malfunctioning. The eyes inexplicably begin to flicker, first off, and then on again. It does this several times, and the scientists become very concerned.

They are all unsure as to what to do following the cloning incident. Paul starts to examine Eyesic, and to see where the trouble might be emanating. They all look on in amazement, and Mr. Stewart begins to speak: "I think it's the cartridge. I can have someone replace it immediately, but what purpose would that serve now?" TC places his hands upon his hips, and lets out a shaken and soft sigh.

A baffled Mr. Stewart leaves the room to locate Michael Kay. Michael is a mechanical scientist who works within the building, and occasionally at different locations assisting in experiments and repairs. He designs the working parts that are installed in most of the cartridges, and power supply.

Nade is finally taken out of the room, unable to be cared for, and leaving only the scientists. At the same time, Mr. Stewart re-enters the room with Michael, and approach

Eyesic. Michael removes the cartridge, and replaces it with another.

They all enter their areas again, and Eyesic is restarted. Unfortunately, the replacement cartridge does not work. Something else is wrong and the cartridge is removed. Michael says to Paul: "I'm leaving it in your hands. My cartridges are not the problem. I think Eyesic needs a little fine tuning."

Paul gives a look of resignation, and motions to TC, and both head back to their laboratory. In their laboratory, Paul begins to check on Eyesic to see what could be causing the trouble. TC looks at him as if he's about to explode, and wants to discuss the captain's motives. Paul just shakes his head, knowing that there is no privacy about talking about such matters.

Just then, the captain enters their laboratory and slowly walks towards the scientists, who stare in disbelief. He states to the scientists emphatically: "The two of you take the rest of the week off, and I'll attend to Eyesic. It will take several days to restore it, and it will have to be tested, again, to make sure it is fully operational." The scientists reluctantly agree, but seem to be transfixed by the captain's presence. There is some sort of strange energy that surrounds him that influences people, and objects that is inexplicable.

Just as abruptly as the captain enters, he exists leaving both scientists wondering what may lie ahead. They both have a deep and unsettling feeling at the pit of their stomachs. They suddenly begin to realize, what may be in store. They do know that from this point on that work, and their lives may never be the same.

For both scientists, the next several days will be spent focusing on their concerns and fears. Also, their focus will be on Eyesic's repairs, and getting a little relaxation. They've decided to use this time for a short vacation since only one experiment can be performed at a time, and there are no others pending.

TC decides to stay at home where he can take it easy in his sprawling, one-level home. It is located in a private and secluded area in Los Panoramas, which is in one of the most beautiful parts of Sacramento, California. His beautiful home has a buff-colored sandstone exterior, and many-spacious rooms. There are many windows that cover nearly the entire façade, along with sliding doors. Most of the interior is in a soft-sky blue.

The back of his home has many windows as well, and a temperature and energy-sensor sliding door leading out to the patio. The entire house is at the height of a two-family home, and seems to tower to the heavens. It's surrounded by lush-green vegetation, flowers, and statues. A stone-path leads to an enchanted forest of more dense flowers, and vegetation to an overlook of grandeur. He's got an incredible 360-degree view. Another path leads to a perfectly-manicured garden that is something right out of Alice in Wonderland. It is a nature-lover's paradise, and truly the American-dream house. Sunsets are spectacular, which bathes the entire area in a soft-golden hue. Tall-flowing trees complete the landscape.

He spends a lot of his time in the backyard sitting in his reclining chair, and staring out into the vastness of this scenic location. Behind him, the ceiling-high windows of his home are like mirrors reflecting the far-off landscape resembling beautiful paintings. While he sits back, wearing his tortoise-shell glasses with silver designs on the edges, the lenses change from clear to dark to accommodate the bright-afternoon sun.

He also enjoys how the setting sun plays amongst the trees casting long shadows across his property, and inside his blue and buff-colored home. It is as though, he is looking beyond the horizon, and to tomorrow passing the stars and beyond. He doesn't seem to have a care in the world sitting on his patio, as he begins bird watching. With his head back and slightly tilted, he watches some barely-visible bird's circling in a clear-blue sky. At that very moment, the sun catches the silver design on the right side of the frame of his glasses making it twinkle like the evening star. There are also shadowy trees, and other far-off sights reflecting off of his glasses.

He watches his surroundings this way until he slowly falls asleep. Within a few hours he awakens. When he tilts his head, again, a faint glow of twilight can be seen gleaming from his glasses. As the day reaches an end, a quaint nightfall slowly seeps in.

Paul spends his free time driving around, and visiting various-information stations. He is looking through The Resource Sections on the Unexplained. He wants information pertaining to his strange experience and encounter. He also uses the linking system, on his Screenview at home, to gather information on similar experiences shared by others like him.

He was never been much of a believer in UFO's, the supernatural or unexplained phenomenon. He does believe, however, that he has encountered something, and it is something he cannot easily explain. Also, since he has not been feeling like himself in the past few days, he is beginning to believe that he has made a strange connection. This connection seems to be something that is otherworldly.

The information he reviews reveals many-extraordinary accounts pertaining to UFO's, and other dimensions. It also includes altered states of consciousness, the supernatural, and miracles. Being that he is not one to attribute his experiences to this type of phenomenon, he would like to have a more concrete, and practical explanation. One search in particular hits very close to home. It mentions rips in time, revealing openings to other dimensions, and beings of these dimensions entering through these rips. There is a sentence that pops out at him that says: "These beings enter into our existence, as we know it, but we are unaware of them."

Paul links the information at the station to his home Screenview, so that he can mull over it when he returns home. He is still, somewhat, in denial and wondering if he really had a paranormal experience. All the while, he can't dismiss the possibility due to the fact of what he has seen, and the feeling of being controlled.

He wants to tell someone of his dilemma, but realizes he cannot. Also, each time he decides he would, he gets an overwhelming sensation of fatigue. It is a fatigue that he cannot overcome, and he then wants to go to sleep.

He spends the remaining time of his short vacation at home. Before returning to work the following week, he continues to review all of the information he has gathered. Still he is unable to accept the reality that something strange, and unexplainable has happened to him. Nor does he have much control over it. Still, he wants to find answers.

CHAPTER 4

On Monday, June 9, 2025 Eyesic's checkup is over, and it's fully operational. On orders from the captain, a few more experiments are performed in the laboratory building and much to the chagrin of the scientists. Several more individuals are cloned successfully.

A top-security laboratory has been set up in California, in the flatlands of the sierra called Las Tierras. This is where the next experiment will take place. This remote, sand-covered area is chosen because the captain wants all of those involved, and the actual experiment kept as secretive as possible. Also, there may be the possibility of radioactivity and other contaminants, and a possibility of genetic and cellular interaction.

There is a single-winding dirt and sand path that leads into this area, surrounded by large-red boulders on either side. It is 11:00 a.m. on a bright and beautiful June afternoon. The brilliant-blue sky is clear with only a few, scattered, fluffy-white clouds drifting by. A mild breeze is blowing, but there is a strange calm in the air.

Suddenly, four, large Magnetic-Energy-Operating Vehicles or MEOV's approach thundering along the path.

They create scattered, swirling-dust clouds as they make their way into this remote area. The vehicles stop at a designated-truck stop indicated by large, bright-green directional arrows imbedded into the ground.

These massive MEOV's are painted steel gray with chemically-energized-magnetic color particles. This special finish enables the vehicles to change color by absorbing the colors within their surroundings, and blend in without being detected. Each vehicle is entitled, Environmental Research Organization with dark-red lettering that can actually break apart. The title appears on both sides, and on top of each vehicle. There is another set of lettering on top of this red lettering that is also energy controlled, and cannot be seen with the naked eye. This special lettering is electromagnetic, and can be controlled on command. It reveals the real name of the experiment, and stays dormant until it is activated.

Ingeniously, the red lettering disappears when another MEOV approaches revealing the actual name of the project. When the red lettering breaks apart, it reveals the capitalized title, PROJECT EYESIC to the other driver, or to a MEOV vehicle flying overhead. It is also displayed on Screenviews within these vehicles that are projected in front of the windshield, and dashboard of each vehicle. Drivers and pilots, seeing this from inside their vehicles, never have to take their eyes from the road or sky. At night or during poor visibility, there are a series of beeps to accompany the Screenviews within the vehicles. They can communicate with each other using this technology, and it is completely undetectable to anyone else. No other type of vehicle can cause this reaction, as this maintains complete secrecy.

A large, bright-red square vehicle speeds around the winding dirt path. It comes to a screeching-abrupt stop next to one of the parked-large vehicles. The engine roars like a lion, and coming out is Captain Meyers, Mr. Stewart, Paul and TC. The captain is dressed in a uniform. He is wearing a red jacket and black pants in full regalia. Paul, TC and Mr. Stewart are dressed in red-protective jumpsuits, and they seem insignificant against the captain.

Captain Meyers exalts a very powerful and intimidating presence. Some of his colleagues feel that he lives a very discreet and almost-reclusive existence because of his position, and caliber. A lot of his past is shrouded in mystery, and he has a very secretive demeanor. Some individuals in the scientific community claim that they do not know where he came from. Nor, do they know what some of his previous assignments have been. Many scientists do know, however, that he is involved when top-secret experiments are conducted. Their belief is that he is very odd and elusive, and otherworldly. His shrouded past only heightens the mystery of the claims, and his former staff have rumored that he doesn't seem to get any older. Although, many do not know much about him, they do know he is the one in charge.

The captain is very cautious, and does not want any unauthorized personnel to know anything about the experiment. Everyone involved have sworn to secrecy for his or her safety, and knowledge of the experiment. Several days before the mention of the experiment, all personnel involved had a tiny patch placed under the skin of their forearm that records their every move.

This patch records specific language that may be uttered that could jeopardize the experiment. All information is recorded, especially words that relate to the experiment: RFactor, Eyesic, people, place and event. The patch also records names of personnel if they are mentioned, changes in body temperature, and bodily rhythms. The pulse rate, blood pressure and stress levels are also measured. It can retain information for quite some time; therefore, it is worn for one month after the experiment, and then removed. This safeguards any information that may be exchanged amongst personnel to their friends or family. Since the captain has to oversee the entire project, he is solely responsible for anything that goes wrong.

A few more MEOV's pull into the area and several men run out wearing black and white uniforms. They have huge cranes that are erected at the site, and begin unloading small-redwood trees that have been uprooted for the experiment.

Several crews begin to set up a huge-gray tent with a transparent-plastic top. It has a clear, horizontal-front panel made of a flexible bubble for viewing. Eyesic and RFactor seem significantly small in comparison to all the vehicles, equipment, and large tent in such a large expanse of space. The tent is equipped with Screenviews, radar, scanners and fusion-generator monitors of all kind. There are energy and light printers, light-operated cameras and solar-powered computers. At 2:15 p.m. everything is set up and ready for the experiment.

The scanners examine the amount of light and energy that comes out of Eyesic's eyes during the experiment, as well as any-surrounding interference that could hamper the outcome. They also scan objects that may be overhead, or beyond to the outermost atmosphere. The sophisticated-sensor system can reach into space, where it can detect objects or interference within the solar system.

The light-sensitive cameras operate solely from light and energy entering into the lens. It then travels through optical cables to a dimensional Screenview. The images, and its surroundings are sent to a vacuum cube were a three-dimensional image appears. This image can either be turned into a print, or place into a computer or stored. This incredible and sensitive-imaging capability can capture a faint star in the night sky. Any available light source can be captured, and the image is always three-dimensional.

Outside of the tent, the crews have laid the small-redwood trees side-by-side against the sunburnt ground. TC and Paul set up Eyesic and RFactor on an experimental table outside of the tent. It is in front of a very wide, white-transparent steel wall. Only Eyesic will be tested before the actual experiment takes place. It is positioned facing the wall.

Diagonally, from this wall is a 3-D screen exactly like the one located in the laboratory, but this one is enormous. There is also a huge-flat rectangular Manifold beside the screen covering an enormous area of ground. Unlike the table in the laboratory, it has no means of support, but just sits flat on the soil. This is where all of the reflected information is sent, and where cloned objects will appear.

Mr. Stewart walks towards the scientist, and places a newly-tested solar cartridge into Eyesic. They all enter the tent along with the many crews, and the captain. This test just measures the brilliance, and motion of the pink-light energy being emitted.

Inside the tent, Paul and TC stand closely together. Paul never tells him about the unshakable feeling, of being controlled, that he has been experiencing for some time. TC senses a change in him, but does not discuss it. TC maintains his composure so no one suspects anything.

Eyesic emits two, deep-pink lights onto the wall that are quite brilliant. The two beams move in unison, in a circular motion against the wall like spotlights. It is the type of pink that if someone looks upon directly, and stares at the white wall next to it, there is an after effect of green. It reaches its' full brilliance and cloning ability, when the light emitted is bright pink. Its light then goes out and the test is complete. Now it is ready for the real thing.

Mr. Stewart and the scientists come out of the tent. Paul and TC reposition their computers in front of the redwood trees, and the 3-D screen.

The Manifold is behind the screen; all is in place, and everyone re-enters the tent.

As Captain Meyer's stands proudly inside the tent, his strong voice gives the command, "Let's go!" TC remotely starts RFactor, and the experiment begins.

RFactor's MCR collects the cells from the trees onto the Skid, as Eyesic's eyes begin to operate. The eyes glow slowly from a deep pink to a bright pink. It then administers two-wide beams of pink-energy light towards the Skid that reflects onto the screen. Incredibly, the small redwoods are cloned onto the Manifold. They are exact right down to their texture, size, color and detail.

Everyone inside the tent is mesmerized, and the captain is ecstatic. The experiment is a success. After a few moments, the captain, Mr. Stewart, and the scientists emerge along with some crew members. Paul and TC begin to wheel their computers back to one of the MEOV's, while checking on them. At the same time, a male technician in the tent suddenly shouts out something inaudible, and then becomes silent peering into a scanner.

Other technicians are checking on their equipment for radioactivity and any abnormalities. About two-minutes later that same technician shouts again: "I'm picking up something on my scanner, and it's also registering beyond the radiation counter." He has everyone in the tent's attention. Paul shouts from outside the tent, "What is it?" The technician replies: "It seems to be some sort of radioactive interference that..." The captain interrupts him yelling: "There should be no interference at this time! The experiment is over! Check you systems again for the source. It's probably here within all of this equipment. I want to be sure of where it's coming from, and not jump to any conclusions." The technician replies: "It's possible that it could be coming from here, but the system shows that it is coming from an outside source. It's not coming from one particular area, but from all over." The captain snaps angrily, "What do you mean all over?" The shaken technician replies: "The scanners aren't registering anything within this area. It's showing up as a large-scattered mass that is passing over, and around this entire area."

Paul, along with TC and the captain, pace around the area, and then separate into different directions. They want to see if anyone or anything may have entered the site. They all stare skyward, as though the summer sky would give them the answer. The entire area seems secure. The crews working outside of the tent, packing up the equipment, are oblivious as to what is going on. They become startled when they see the scientists looking around, as though something is happening.

Paul suddenly reaches for his forehead with his right palm and squints, as though he has suddenly gotten a terrible headache. TC and the Captain walk towards him to make sure he is alright. TC with much concern asks, "Paul, are you okay?" The captain has a look of concern and suspicion, reiterating TC's words. Paul collects himself and says, "It's nothing, I..." He hesitates and continues: "I just feel a little dizzy. I'm fine. I'm fine. It's probably just the equipment. I'm fine now." They walk him over to a small boulder, sitting him down to rest a moment. TC and the captain look at each other suspiciously; they believe that there may be something wrong with him.

The same technician again cries out: "Wait, the signals are getting weak now. Whatever it was has just disappeared. It must be far out in space. I'm not getting any more interference."

Everyone remain silent waiting for the captain's next command and instructions. The captain, somewhat dismayed asks in a loud voice, "Space?" He continues, "I don't know who or what is trying to interfere with the experiment. If there were any interference and it just disappeared, then it is coming from an unknown source." He turns to the technician and asks begrudgingly: "Where in space did this mass come from, and where did it head? I want to see the mass that you picked up on your scanner immediately."

The technician displays a 3-D image for the captain. He seems interested, as though it is something familiar to him. He says to himself: "This illustrates the mass has come from an area in the Virgo Cluster." He does not give out any information, but says to the technician: "I'm going to have to look into this further. There will be no more experiments. I, hereby, postpone any future experiments until I meet with my officials." He then says out of the corner of his mouth: "These people don't what they are up against." Then he shouts: "Let's clean up and clear out of here!"

He heads to his vehicle and shouts to all the crews: "Get those vehicles ready, and get those trees and equipment out of here!" Turning to the scientist he continues shouting: "Get those computers back to the laboratory, and clear this area!" The captain's attitude seemed to change, but he is just pretending to be very worried. It is as though he knows something, as if who or what that has interfered isn't welcomed.

All of the equipment is reloaded onto the vehicles, and the last of the crew, and the men in special uniforms are aboard. The MEOV's leave the flatlands, and cruise along steadily in their organized caravan. They are like linked boxcars from an old circus proceeding one after the other. Just moments later, it is as though they were never there, and an experiment had never taken place.

They are also leaving a cool hideaway: a great area for someone looking for a getaway, where they can never be found. It is a place of vastness: an open plain, spacious skies, boulders, and mountains as a backdrop. Again, the air is calm on this sunny-late afternoon. Just as it began, it ends with only swirling-dust clouds as a reminder.

The next day Tuesday, June 10th, Paul is with TC, their staff, and some of the technicians from the experiment. They are in a briefing room at the laboratory and research building. Paul and TC are seated at opposite ends of a long-black shiny table. Everyone else fill in the spaces that remain. In the middle of the table are cellular-molecular wafer implants. They will use these to communicate with the captain, during the briefing.

As TC listens to the staff's conversation, Paul reads the Screenview being displayed next to him. A look of horror comes upon his face. He mumbles aloud: "There have been strange sightings in various states of California. People have reported being disturbed by flying objects high in the sky, and experiencing some strange-unknown force."

He is shocked and cannot believe it. He motions with his lips to TC, "Look at this. See this?" TC looks at the Screenview and only sees advertisements. With a look of surprise on his face, and not wanting to interrupt their staff he quietly asks, "See what Paul?" Paul is confused and answers softly, "This!" He then points at the Screenview and whispers, "These sightings and experiences!" TC asks half-jokingly and audibly: "Man, what are you talking about? What sightings?" Paul is dumbfounded. He is not sure whether TC is being funny, or if he's being serious. Paul asks again: "You don't see this? It's headline news." Looking closely at TC, he begins to get a deep and unsettling feeling, as he realizes he's very serious. TC then says to him: "You should see a doctor. I don't think you're doing well since the experiment yesterday. You should schedule an appointment right away!" There is a deafening silence in the room.

Paul is motionless and embarrassed, and just stares at everyone. He is cautioned by one of his staff, as to what this could do to his reputation. With a defeated look upon his face, Paul's heart beats fast, and his mouth becomes dry. He nervously licks his lips, and tries to convince the staff by reading more of the story.

As he starts to read aloud, all eyes are upon him. He desperately tries to convince everyone that what he is reading is real. Paul begins: "The news states that many people in several cities in California, and small towns in Nevada, and as far as Washington State have reported strange incidences. There were small-earth tremors and vibrations, and rumbling sounds all around. There is also a constant feeling of uneasiness for many, as though being watched. There have also been sightings of small-gray objects hovering far up in the sky. No man-made aircraft or weather phenomenon have been proven to be the cause, or could have demonstrated such an event. The objects didn't make any sound whatsoever. Several other dark objects were seen moving slowly across the sky, and became visually clearer when passing a cloud. They appeared to some like tiny-gray balloons, and to others like mist forming. Those flying in air vehicles stated it left a misty film on their vehicles windows, as though hot air was being blown against it. It then turned into a rust-colored powder hindering their view. Some saw various-tiny specks swirling in the air. Another group of people reported they think it had to do with an experiment conducted yesterday. Many believe that this happening is extraterrestrial in nature, with the help of several-secret authorities."

Paul stops reading and cries out: "So it did leak out that we did the experiment. It doesn't say what the experiment was for or who witnessed it." He looks around the room, and again, all eyes are upon him. TC blurts out, "There's nothing there

Paul," trying to snap him back into reality. He continues: "I think you need to see a doctor at once."

The fearful staff members and technicians get up slowly, and quickly walk out of the room in disbelief. TC has great concern for Paul, but his attention gets thwarted when a message signal comes through Screenview from the captain.

TC reaches over and takes a wafer implant from the table, and places it inside his ear. He listens and talks quietly to the captain. He begins: "This is TC. How are you sir?" As TC speaks, he walks away from the table, and out of earshot of Paul. He quietly discusses what Paul has just read, and the incident that has just occurred.

Paul stares at him, but, again becomes absorbed in what he is reading. A few moments later, the captain insists on speaking to Paul. TC points to the wafers, and Paul appearing quite worried, quietly picks up the conversation. TC is disconnected from the conversation, as Paul inserts the wafer into his ear.

The captain is furious, and questions Paul about what he had just read to the staff. He berates him, as to whether he was trying to make a mockery of the entire-scientific community. Paul is at a loss for words, and does not know how to relate what he has just read. To him it is reality, and as clear as day. He cannot give the captain any answers or explanation.

In his ear, the captain loudly shouts: "You are suspended, and you won't be able to perform any experiments, or enter the laboratory at all. You are not allowed to return to work without my permission, or enter the laboratory without my permission. When I allow permission, you are to enter with an escort. I'm placing you under a physician's care. If for any reason you enter this building, you will be kept in closed quarters."

The captain suspects that Paul has somehow gained some communicated insight into the unknown, and he must take control of it. He has a hidden agenda for Paul that is unbeknownst to TC, or the rest of the staff. Paul, in total disbelief says to TC flatly, "I have to leave!" Without another word, he removes the wafer and leaves the briefing room. He heads home to await further orders from the captain.

TC is again talking to the captain, and he is ordered not to have any communications with Paul, until he is told. TC wants to know what transpired between the two, but the captain will not give any details, and they both say goodbye.

Before Paul can make it to his vehicle in the garage, he notices three people watching him. They are at a distance standing next to a dark-purple vehicle. As he briefly takes his eyes off of them and enters his vehicle, the purple vehicle is already pulling up beside him. He looks over to lock eyes with the driver, and the person on the passenger side. To his unpleasant surprise, he cannot see their faces. Somehow, they are shadowed in a well-lit garage, but he can make out silhouettes of what seem to be males. They turn in his direction, but all he can see are angles and shapes of what may be their faces. He is quite unnerved by their odd appearance. Suddenly, he feels a powerful sense of dread and a strong surge of adrenaline being forced through him. It's as though his life may be on the line.

They appear to him as if he is in a dream, and this makes the situation seem hazy. It doesn't seem they want anything from him, but just to observe. He is unsure as to why he cannot clearly see them, or if it's they do not want to be seen.

Paul turns away to pull out of the garage, and as he does, the vehicle quickly and strangely gets ahead of him. He looks through the vehicle's-rear window to see if he can make out anything that may seem familiar to him. As both vehicles head towards the highway, he starts to think about what took place earlier with the captain. He envisions what he saw on Screenview, and thinks he may be seeing things before they happen.

As the purple vehicle continues in front of him, he begins to get a better view in the daylight of the strange-individuals inside. The three of them appear like men, but misshapen, and undefined. He can partially see through all of them, as if he was looking through fabric or material, but they are not transparent. At that very moment, all-three individuals in the vehicle turn in unison, and look behind them in his direction. Paul is quite alarmed, and wants to change lanes to hurry past them. He signals and veers off to the right, and at that very moment, the vehicle does the same. As it does, it changes from purple to silver, and nearly transparent. He is now quite startled. As it changes color and lanes, it physically goes through another vehicle without affecting it.

Being a scientist and understanding the laws of physics, he is at a total loss as to what he is seeing. The vehicle turns back to purple, and continues on its course. Paul says to himself, "The captain must have sent them."

It has become quite difficult for Paul to concentrate on the road, without taking his eyes off the vehicle. Suddenly, the driver reaches out of the window with some narrow appendage, and points skyward. Paul looks in the direction of the pointing, and it leads him directly to the sun. On the other side of the sky, is a pale-daytime full moon. This has no meaning for him, but he knows it must be something significant, and related to something cosmic. He thinks to himself: "If it involves the sun, it may be something planetary. I wonder if it is solar flares or an eclipse."

The purple vehicle then begins to slowly fade into something that Paul cannot see. It is an invisible-vanishing point on the highway. As only the rear window and trunk remain, Paul strains to understand. In a matter of seconds it is gone, and so is any explanation. When Paul finally arrives home, he doesn't leave or communicate with anyone.

CHAPTER 5

On Saturday, June 14th, the captain has ordered Paul to come to the laboratory and research building to meet with him, and a physician. When he arrives, he is escorted to a designated-consultation room. It is small, but consists of a rectangular table and six chairs, two on either side, and one on each end. The captain and an unknown man greet him. He is seated at one end of the table, while the captain and the unknown man are seated to his left. Paul is asked a barrage of questions, and is told that he will not be able to perform any future experiments until his mind is deemed lucid. He is also startled to learn that he will not be able to have any communication with laboratory staff, which includes TC, or anyone.

The captain says to him: "I feel we need to have this consultation because, I am concerned about your recent behavior. I want to discuss your reaction to the experiment, and some other issues. I feel that you may have some insight or special gift. Let's just say, a certain ability that could either help, or hinder future experiments. I want to start out with a few routine questions and as we progress, we'll have a clearer understanding in each session.

In his confusion Paul asks: "I thought I was here to see a physician?" The captain gives him a look that solidifies that he has been deceived, and coerced into something bigger than he could have ever imagined. Paul interrupts exasperated, "Each session?" The captain says coarsely, "Yes, each session!" Paul says astonished: "I thought that's why I came here, and that would be it! I was willing to see a doctor, but I don't see why I need sessions with you." The captain looks at him awkwardly, and then looks over his left shoulder at the man sitting beside him and says: "This is Foster. He will assist me during these sessions by gathering data, and storing the information."

As the captain says this, Foster takes out a small, flat-octangular device. Sitting on top of this device is a glossy, black, convex-glass projection. This projection is a lens, which sends enlarged images to a computer. On the back of the lens is a gray covering, which mounts it to the device. It is an imaging recorder for body statistics, electromagnetic-energy sensing, and unusual-sound waves. It is also for detecting any foreign or extraterrestrial energy, if any is present.

The captain asks questions such as Paul's whereabouts prior to the experiment, and if he had any unusual or unexplainable experiences prior to the experiment. He asks a series of questions regarding whether Paul possesses any psychic abilities, or of any sort of experience where he would have used an extra sense.

As the session continues, the captain orders Paul to tap into his so-called gift. He wants him to find out how he could have received the unseen information shown to him on Screenview. Paul looks coldly toward Foster and the captain, and is speechless. He looks down towards the table, then looks up and says stoically: "I don't have any ability. I just read what I saw. I'd rather be thought of as crazy, than to think I have some special ability. I just looked at the report and there it was, as clear as day. I don't know, maybe it was a fluke. I have no power of any kind, and no gift. This questioning is pointless. Is that what this is all about?" Paul becomes more agitated and gets up, as though to leave, and is ordered to sit back down. The captain has a long list of questions that he wants to ask, and Paul is making it exceptionally difficult for him to continue. He sits back down, and becomes tightlipped refusing to answer any more questions. This enrages the captain.

The captain rises up from his chair, and pounds his fist on the table sending a loud bang echoing throughout the sealed room. He points angrily and says: "I've seen powers like this before, and you cannot withhold this type of information from me. I am well aware of these abilities in some individuals.

121

This type of ability can change the course of history, not to mention, make future experiments foolproof. You have no idea what your powers could do. What you have, from where I come is called..." The captain catches himself beginning to reveal too much.

Paul realizes there is really something otherworldly about the captain. He starts to think that his ability is actually a threat, and maybe it endangers something that only the captain knows. His mind begins to race, and he has a stunning realization that he's exhibiting some sort of otherworldly-competitive ability. This could be why the captain is trying so fiercely to intimidate him. The ability must be something that is controlled by some sort of outside entity. Slowly, things are starting to come together.

The captain continues: "From this day forward, I am going to test your abilities, like I am right now." He then sits down, and regains his composure. A look of confusion, anger, and fear covers Paul's face, as he tries to comprehend this ability. The captain sighs, and takes a deep breath then continues: "I want you to have a short stay here in the laboratory. I have set up a room for you which will accommodate your every need. Starting now, when this session has ended, you will report to your room and stay there for the duration of these sessions. You will have a Screenview and full meals: clothing, deliveries, fresh linens, and various recreations to keep you busy. You will have visits by appointed staff that will be timed. You not are allowed to leave the building, or go anywhere on these grounds unaccompanied."

The session comes to a close and the captain, and security personnel escort Paul to his room. He immediately resists. Suddenly, he feels compelled by some controlling-unseen force that makes him go quietly. He now knows for sure that there is something very strange about the captain. There is now an overpowering energy that he cannot resist, when he is in the captain's presence. Although, this does not cause him to become easily influenced, and manipulated.

There will be only but a few who will have interaction with Paul while he is detained here. TC has no knowledge that any of this is taking place. He has been told that Paul has taken a leave-of-absence for the time being, and relocated until further notice. He will return when he is deemed fit for work. TC believes this to be true, and doesn't have any inkling that something-quite disturbing is taking place to his colleague. He would like to know about Paul's well-being, but does not dare question the captain's authority.

Paul is shocked by this treatment, and enters his room with consternation. He looks back at the captain like a helpless animal being placed in a cage. He feels betrayed and bewildered, as he cannot believe the turn-of-events. He yells at the captain: "You're not human just like everyone has said. I've heard people say that you are otherworldly, and I believe it. That is why no one knows where you came from, and what you did in the past.

He is placed in his room, and the door is sealed shut. The sound of the door closing resonates down the corridor. The captain's voice is in his room, as he talks through the door. He says: "You have no idea who I am, or where I come from, and how far I can go. My intentions are to make people think that this is an alien invasion, it is not. What it will be is determined by how I can get your kind to betray one another. This in turn will give me ultimate power in the end, because many will lose hope. I have already set the wheels in motion, starting with one of your fellow scientists. He was the first one to betray you. This cycle will continue worldwide. Yet most of the time, it will be as subtle as your wind blows. It is already being incorporated into your technology, and will be implanted into every-living cell of your kind. There is no way of stopping this. This will be the ultimate power that will be assisting in the betrayal. It has been included in the construction of your computer from day one, and right under your nose. It is so minute that it has gone unnoticed. It is called Element G by your authorities. In time, you will hear about this." The security staff escorts the captain down the corridor, and they all disappear around a corner.

As ordered by the captain, all future-scientific experiments that have been scheduled for Eyescic and RFactor have been canceled. Meanwhile, they remain locked and monitored in the laboratory near the area where they were assembled.

During the next work week, as the laboratory workers go about their shifts, they are all somewhat nervous. They don't know exactly why two-unused computers need monitoring. All they know, however, is to report any disturbances to officials immediately. The computers will be monitored in their room by the same surveillance as the rest of the laboratory, until they are ready to perform their next experiment.

TC has been commissioned to start on another project, while he awaits the outcome of RFactor and Eyesic. Although, for the time being assigned to another laboratory within the building, he has a lot of free time on his hands. He spends a lot of it doing research at home, and thinking of Paul. He is feeling some guilt, as though he is responsible for his temporary dismissal. He has thoughts of making amends, as soon as he has contact with him.

Meanwhile, Paul is confined to his room, and is sitting at a small table interacting with a game. His room has no real comforts of home. There are no pictures on the walls, and the walls are covered in a copper-colored film that reflects like a mirror. He has a full-size bathroom and a kitchen area. Natural light enters through a series of mirrors and ducts on the walls, and ceiling. One large-open duct on the ceiling is a faux skylight that is designed to look like a gentle-blue sky, with diffused-clouds scattered throughout. This lighting also reflects off the wall coverings, and fills the room with a glow. There are things to keep him occupied and four-dimensional games attached to the Screenview. Other items are for his amusement, but there are no means of communication. An audio display on the table is playing soft music, and he is trying to make the best of this awful situation. On another wall is a magnetized, time-day display with temperature that functions by airflow, and energized polarity.

The next several days will be trying for him, as he is still questioned by the captain pressing him for information.

A few days later on June 18th, it is a typical day in the laboratory building. The computers are still locked away in their room. They are kept this way, until the day turns into a wonderful and splendorous evening. This particular evening is cool, dark, clear and starry. It can make any stargazer's imagination run wild to lean back and look into the heavens, and see far out into the universe. There are shooting stars, planets, constellations and the like. With the heavens being so vast, in this unobstructed area, the laboratory building appears as a black-rectangular silhouette along the horizon. It sits like a ruin of a bygone era. It resembles that of one-last remaining fortress, forgotten by time with a backdrop of a star-sprinkled evening sky.

On this evening, the building seems unusually quiet and strange. All of the workers inside are gone. The darkened room where the computers are stationed, they sit upon an examination table facing a window. The bright-highway lighting in the distance begins illuminating a bluish hue onto the building, through the window, and onto the computers. The room is sparse with the exception of items on a counter, and on some shelves. There are some aprons hanging upon the wall that look as though, they are not often used. The highway lights plays upon the objects in the room making each appear to be centuries old. All the while, motionless, like monuments built to stand the test of time. Perhaps, they are waiting for someone or something to give them life, so they can tell a story or two.

Also, in a frighteningly-chilling way Eyesic looks alive. The illumination reflects off its hooded eyes, staring straight ahead, like that of a cat peering in the darkness. It appears almost human, but forever in a trance. Its large, dark-oval-shaped head seems disembodied from what should be shoulders going downward. It is quite a strange sight.

As Paul spends another restless evening in his room, he looks at the time display, which shows 7:30 p.m. He decides to watch Screenview, and interact with a modular game from his bed. He watches for a while, and actually lose track of time. When he checks the time again, it is 9:48 p.m. He decides to call it a night, and tosses the game across the room to a table. It misses, and hits the edge of the table making a loud-boom sound, echoing around the room. It also makes a splattering sound as it hits the floor. Afterwards, there's a long-loud silence that permeates the room.

When Paul gets up to pick up the game, he feels a strange pain in his forehead. He reaches for his forehead, and slowly backs up towards his bed, and sits back down. He becomes concerned, and has thoughts of what has taken place before, and wonders what will happen now. He begins to feel unsettled, and knows something is happening.

128

As he sits on the bed, he hears a strange-humming sound. Unable to tell if it is coming from within his room or from outside, he looks around puzzled, and tries to remain calm. The humming seems to be getting louder and louder, as though it is being turned up in volume. The sound is consistent, and becomes a vibrating and piercing noise that he can actually feel within. It jars him inside like that of an invasive-rude awakening.

There is also a crackling sound like stiff paper being crumpled. Paul places his hands over his ears, and then removes them thinking this might thwart the sound. He is thinking this must be his imagination, and he shakes his head in disbelief. He wonders where it's originating, and if there is anyone in the building, or if anyone else can hear it.

He paces back and forth in the room like a caged tiger, then walks towards the exit door. He wipes his hand across the panel, as if this would free him from the room, which has sealed his fate within the laboratory. As he swipes, he suddenly senses a strange-unsettling presence within the room. There is a sound of a large pop, and he becomes terribly frightened. He has no one to communicate with, nor can he leave his room.

While holding his hand against the door panel, his palm begins to perspire. His heart begins pounding in his chest, and in his ears. The strange pain returns to his forehead, and the overwhelming sense of being controlled returns. He turns around in horror, and there standing in his room is something that seems to be not from this world. It is a misshapen being like the dark images he encountered in the garage. This being is grainy and semi-transparent, and stands six-foot five inches tall. There are no striking features at all such as eyes, nose or mouth. It looks one dimensional and lightweight, as if moving through time and space. Paul is able to look partially through random points of this being, and see lighted objects on the other side of the room. The texture is like that of very-refined particleboard or sandpaper. The being is moving like living cells seen under a microscope.

As this is taking place inside, on the outside of the building in the night sky, something else is happening. There is a round, bright-orange glowing object hovering above. It is silent and still, as though waiting for something or someone. Suddenly, the object administers a large band of white light upon the building. It puts everything functioning within the building, and the surrounding area in a catatonic state. Paul and the computers are the only things completely unaffected.

Paul is terrified and motionless. He has not moved from the spot from which he is standing. As he stares through the being, he begins to have a realization. He sees himself on the outside of the building witnessing the strange event that is taking place. He is also being shown the answers to the questions that are inside of his head. Though he is not thinking of such things, he is controlled to believe that he is. The knowledge seems to be coming directly from the strange sensation in his forehead.

In a split second, he is conspicuously back in his room with this being that does not speak, but causes him to be afraid, and have strange visions. Paul tries to make sense of the sighting thinking that the being is talking to him through his mind. Then, he realizes that this is not the case because there is no comprehensible communication. He can only understand information and not send it, as there is just realization. It is as though the answers have already been there and now they are emerging, because of the being's presence. Paul now knows that the pain he has been getting in his forehead is actually a device that has been placed there for knowledge.

He also realizes that the being is actually not there to harm him, but to warn him. He has knowledge that there are other beings already there, from an area in space called the Virgo Cluster. These beings are not benevolent, and have been unleashed to cause chaos all over the world. Paul realizes that this being is also from the Virgo Cluster, but is not hostile like the others, who have already begun to start a chain reaction.

Paul sees the bottle of solution that spilled on his jacket, and how it was instrumental in bringing about this particular, and current encounter. He sees the discovery of Element G, and how it is a foreign material with many uses, especially as a genetic-communication tool. He also becomes aware of his experience with the purple vehicle on the highway, and the sun and is given their meaning. Paul feels that he is the chosen one, and given all of the answers.

The realization also shows him of that afternoon, during his drive to the laboratory, when he saw the gray object in the sky. He understands the flash and the pain in his forehead. It was the moment he had entered time, and space that is shared with other beings that exist on a mental plane. These beings can only identify with one another, and track others through mental tags, when on a physical plane. Since Paul did not contain this data, it was placed within him. It is the area that can function without the use of the physical body, and beyond the normal senses, his brain. Element G is the key to his connection. This is how it is designed to be used, once it makes contact with a living being. This experience is showing him something that seems divine, and that something on a larger scale is taking place. Also, his ability to see into the future will involve things that only he will know. These things will be resolved at a given time and place in the future.

While this realization is happening, the object outside has caused a reaction to occur in the room where the computers are located. The room suddenly fills with low light, and Eyesic has taken on a life of its' own. Its' eyes begin to enlighten, as though programmed by some invisible force. They become brighter and brighter, from pink to deep pink reaching full brilliance. Then, two, pink-energy beams of light are emitted.

Eyesic begins to turn from side to side upon the table, as if by unseen hands. It moves slowly and deliberately, and peers around the room as if searching for something. It rotates around, and notices RFactor next to it on the table. As it peers at it, it suddenly becomes motionless, and cannot take its' eyes off of the other computer. Then, within a split second, the eyes go out completely, and the room is dark. A few seconds later, a quick-pink blast is released. There is a frying, crackling and popping sound similar to cold water being sprayed on burning-hot metal.

The room again fills with low light, as the operating mechanisms on RFactor make a low-sizzling sound as it melts away. Eyesic uses its' energy light as weapons and nearly destroys all of RFactor leaving just parts of The Skid. It then moves slowly across the table, and levitates into midair moving slowly around the room. It seems to be getting its bearing as to where it is. Moving back to the table, it hovers over RFactors remains, and places itself upon The Skid becoming one computer.

The black coloring of Eyesic engulfs the remains, and there is no longer any trace of RFactor. All of the components and capabilities have now become one completely-transformed computer with, seemingly, some unknown-sinister purpose. There is a soft-pink glow surrounding the merged computers. With another bright-pink flash, they both disappear into nothingness. Beneath the window in the room where the computers were before disappearing, a large-black void has appeared. In an instant, it too disappears.

The being that had so frightened Paul has also begun to dissipate before his eyes. Paul doesn't want to believe what has just taken place. There are no communication devices to connect him to the outside world, where he can share his experience. There is only an emergency-medical panel on the wall. It is here, where he can look into or just place his hand, and instantly receive help or medication. Only, in an actual emergency will an automated-medical attendant be activated.

As everything around him returns to normal, he knows this extraordinary experience is why he has been confined to this room. He walks towards the foot of his bed dazed wondering if he's in a dream. Not sure of anything anymore, he looks at the time, which is now 10:18 p.m. He shakily sits across his bed, sliding himself backward towards the head of the bed, and quickly falls asleep.

The object above the building darts up and out into the night sky. It has disappeared just like the computers. Everything goes back to normal in the building, and the surrounding area. The laboratory's surveillance has returned, and has registered the missing computers.

Their whereabouts are now the sole responsibility of Captain Meyers. He is instantly notified by linked-technology systems of their disappearance. He has the disappearance investigated immediately, and quickly relays this information to Jim Harrison. He asks Jim to quietly look into it, and Jim is ecstatic. In his feeble mind, a diabolical scenario is beginning to take shape. As he knows what went into the computers construction, he believes this secret investigation may turn out to make him famous. Maybe now, he can finally get his due and revenge. Unknown to the captain, Jim is planning to send this information to the news media so the disappearances will be made public.

The next morning, June 19th at 8:00 a.m., there are various authorities scattered everywhere along the laboratory and research building complex. The media rush in on the anonymous tip they received from Jim. They scurry up and around the laboratory's hill, and surround the building. All are unable to enter the building due to the powerful-energy field.

This impermissible information goes over all technological sound systems: Interstellar broad spectrums and Screenviews. News media from everywhere have joined in. With all of the coverage of the story, it has come down to basically, sharing the same information. Screenview announcements and on news links cautions: "These computers are very dangerous, and possibly, radioactive and should not be tampered with. Everyone should just stay away and be cautious. If someone sees something suspicious or unusual, they should report it to their local authorities." Various spins are added by the panicked media from its take on the incident. This is adding unnecessary, and unsubstantiated, fuel to an already-distorted fire.

Immediately approaching, in his red vehicle, is Captain Meyers, who is in full regalia. He has learned that the media received information, through an anonymous source about this serious incident. His authoritative demeanor, therefore, seems to represent that he needs to properly investigate the matter.

He is stoic and pretentious. Albeit, quite upset and angry, he is concealing it with his serious facade.

Undeterred by the spectacle, he walks up to the other authorities and reporters without a word, and scans the area. As he does not know the extent of information received by the media, or the source, he fiercely guards his actions as the situation unfolds. This puts him in a precarious situation, as he does not want to appear not knowing all of what is taking place. Nor, does he want to reveal that he had no control over the leaked information.

As the captain enters the building, more authorities arrive at the laboratory. There are hordes of news media. The captain mischievously smiles before entering the building. Thoughts enter his head of the irony of the whole situation. He does not have to worry about anyone entering the building to investigate, as they are unable to do so, or find out about Paul.

As the media are unable to enter the building, they try to gather information from staff, and the authorities and overheard chatter. TC is here also, on orders from the captain, and is caught up in the commotion. Shouts begin to fill the air about the disappearance of dangerous computers. He looks around trying to hear what is going on. Someone shouts aloud: "The computers are gone, and have disappeared without a trace. I think the scientists who created these computers are to blame." The man shouting is named Gus, and he is not a staff member, nor has he worked with Eyesic or RFactor. He is actually an old colleague of Jim Harrison, who has orchestrated this scenario to bring more attention to the incident. By placing all of the emphasis on Gus, Jim believes that this will help divert any blame that may be placed upon him by the captain. It will also allow him to bide some time to concoct a story about Element G, and its relationship to the disappearance of the computers. He hopes he can point fingers and become a hero.

The authorities ask questions-upon-questions before the previously-asked questions have been fully answered. Another important figure is Authority Personnel, Mr. Kerns. He is a tall, comical-looking man with auburn hair with blonde highlights. He walks over to Captain Meyers, who has just exited the building. He asks him quietly: "Were there any signs of breaking and entering? No one could have done something like this without leaving a clue behind." The captain glances at him and says a resounding, "No!" Mr. Kerns continues: "Was there even the slightest bit of evidence: a fingerprint, footprint, debris? Was there anything? Any marks on the doors or windows to show if anyone used force to get in?" The captain does not speak. He stares at Mr. Kerns and replies: "My people are working on this. It's a matter of a higher authority. You, along with your men and women should not be here. You were notified by the media..." Before he finishes his sentence, Gus begins to shout out again about the computers. The captain becomes incensed. He looks at Gus and demands that Mr. Kerns remove him immediately, as he is not employed by the Laboratory. The captain, again, reenters the building leaving Mr. Kerns to ponder whether he should continue being there. He wonders if he should have asked the questions that he had.

As he sets about fulfilling the captain's request, he notices Gus is already out of his reach. Gus quickly makes his way to his vehicle, as he does not want to be identified. He fears being captured for his knowledge. He speeds away before Mr. Kerns has a chance to pursue him.

The media gets out of hand with the situation, and relates the disappearance to all sorts of strange phenomenon. Nearly all media reports state that no one or nothing has been caught. Most accounts state: "There are no witnesses, and no one is under suspicion." Within a half-an-hour, the massive crowds begin to thin out. There is no one in charge to give out any information, and nothing else seems forthcoming. The area soon clears out.

More workers continue entering the building joining those inside, who are on the alert. They are asking questions to each other, and it just sounds like voices over voices. The officials and scientists are concerned that too much publicity on this disappearance will cause a sensation or, a nation-wide panic.

Inside the building, the captain along with TC and their staff enter a viewing area with a Screenview. Together, they view the images picked up from the infrascreens, from the room where the computers were stored. The images are very dark with huge amounts of static-electricity everywhere. There is a lot of rotating movement of some kind, and several-pink flashes of beams of light. Suddenly, there is a huge-light display. Then, there is nothing to be seen, and everything goes black.

As the captain begins speaking to everyone, he tries to convey a sense of innocence in regards to the situation. He begins: "This incident that has taken place is something I have never experienced. This seems to be some sort of phenomenon that requires further scientific investigation. As scientists, we've studied different realms of existence. We have studied matter, and how things work or don't work. We have not come across anything visually or physically, as to what we've just witnessed.

There has been no substantial-scientific proof that matter may be able to dematerialize, or travel across time and space until now. I don't have all the answers. It is as though those computers came alive, and just simply vanished into thin air. I am not taking any questions, as I don't have any answers. I will discuss all of what has happened with my people. I will issue a statement to the media, and let them know the situation is under control. There is no danger to anyone." TC and the others just stare at each other in disbelief. They dare not question the captain, and leave the room.

The captain contacts his media liaison through the Screenview, who issues a report to the media. The statement released claims: "The earlier reports were due to sensationalism, and the truth is that only a burglary had occurred. There is no danger to anyone. The incident is ruled a theft." No further commentary is issued.

While the captain remains in the building, he quietly enters Paul's room, and quickly shuts the door. Paul is in bed watching Screenview, and sits up slowly. He is surprised to see the captain who says, "Don't get up." He sits at the table, and begins questioning Paul. He demands: "I want to know what happened last night." Paul is apprehensive. He is unable to figure out how the captain could possibly know what he had experienced. "I don't know what you mean," Paul replies. The captain says sternly: "You know the answer just like you have before."

The captain continues: "I know you leaked the computers disappearance to the media, and I want to know how. I'm sure you have some knowledge, as they were kept not too far from this section of the laboratory." Paul, rising slowly, becomes incensed and declares, "I know nothing of this." His voice rises: "What are you talking about? When did this happen?"

The captain turns to the Screenview, and Paul looks at him lowering his eyes. "I want you to read this, and what the report says," the captain demands. Paul trembles and stammers, as he fears the captain knows of his experience. He reluctantly watches the news and states in shock: "It says a computer used for scientific experiments have disappeared." He also interprets: "An event will take place, not far from this laboratory building, concerning someone named Anne Welch. She will be in this very building being questioned about events that have happened to her." The captain asks, "Is that's right?" Paul doesn't want to read any further into the story and asks: "How can this be? How do I know this? What are you doing to me?" His ability seems unbelievable to him, but the captain is not moved. Paul feels that he is just a small piece of a gigantic puzzle being constructed by the captain. He wants a way out of it.

The captain's says: "I see that your ability, to see into the future, is structured around events concerning the computers. The captain then turns off the Screenview, and exits the room.

Paul is left baffled and infuriated, and goes to use the bathroom. He throws water onto his face, and gazes into the mirror. He stares at his reflection, as though he no longer recognizes himself. Over the next-few days, and against his will, he will no longer have to read to see into the future. Just the captain's very presence will now cause this reaction within him.

CHAPTER 6

On June 26th, Paul's foresight becomes a reality. On a warm afternoon at 5:03 p.m., something strange is happening in the town below the laboratory. In the living room of a middle-class home, a Screenview is showing movies to a young man with his feet upon the coffee table. His mother enters the living room from the kitchen, and yells at him to get his feet off of the furniture. She then returns to the kitchen. Her name is Anne Welch. She is a small woman no more than 110-pounds, and always seems to be in some kind of frenzy. At 41-years old, she looks many years beyond her age. Her close-cropped blond hair is unkempt and rarely styled. She doesn't wear a stitch of make-up on her very-fair pale complexion, and has a constant appearance of someone sickly.

Anne suffers from allergies too, especially hay fever, which leaves her with reddened-watery eyes. Regardless of her outward appearance, she is always cheery and outgoing. Her son, Bert, is a comical 17-year old who is a little gawky with a freckled face. He jumps up and shuts off the Screenview, and enters the kitchen where Anne is preparing dinner. He looks at what she is preparing and says: "I'm going to Ron's house. I'll be back later." His mother nods, and goes about her cooking.

The house is quiet, and there is only the sound of food sizzling in pots. A burst of steam lifts the lid from one of the pots. A frothy-stream trickles down the side spilling onto the polished cooktop.

As Anne cooks, she leans over the sink and looks out the window through sheer-white-lacy curtains. They hang low, and gently brush the sill just over the kitchen sink. She has an unobstructed view into the surrounding neighborhood. There are large trees in her backyard that cast long-dark afternoon shadows throughout the property, and across the driveway that she can also see.

While she goes about her cooking, there is a very-bright flash of pink light. It flashes across the window and pours through the curtains. It looks as though a large vehicle of some kind is backing in, but then disappears. Anne strains herself for a better look. She parts the curtains, but sees nothing. Absent-mindedly thinking it is her husband arriving home early, she calls out, "Who's there, is that you honey?" It is not her husband. She mumbles aloud: "Hmm, maybe it's one of the neighbor's vehicles."

She then goes back to her cooking, and a puzzled look comes over her face. "Something is peculiar," she thinks.

Then she says aloud: "That's strange. I shouldn't be able to see any vehicle lights this brightly, not in broad daylight."

Suddenly, the pink light flashes by the window again. This time she does not part the curtains, but just stands against the cooktop staring in the direction of the window. Still, she doesn't see nor hear anything and says, "How peculiar!" Feeling uneasy, and turning away from the window, she looks around the kitchen wondering what is going on. Looking back out the window again, she senses something behind her.

There is a tingling sensation all over her body, as the hairs on the back of her neck stand straight up. Her heart beats heavily in her chest; as fear grips her, she has a heightened sense of awareness. Suddenly, feeling in terrible danger, she turns completely around and there is Eyesic. Its deep pink eyes are staring directly at her, as it's engulfed in a black mist from its' oval head downwards. Joined with RFactor, it is now a ghastly specter similar to a hooded figure. Anne is panic-stricken, but before she could scream or move, it fires. There is a wide beam of deep-pink energy blasted onto her entire body. The room is filled with a warm-pink glow, and Anne is completely engulfed.

Unlike what Eyesic is programmed to do, which is cloning, it instead seems to have had no effect on her. Eyesic's

146

eyes enlightening in pink again, and it quickly vanishes from the room. Everything returns to normal. Anne remains standing in the same spot for several seconds, and then looks around the room coming out of a daze. With no recollection of what has just happened to her, she returns to cooking.

Several minutes later, still having no memory of what has happened, she starts to feel very unusual. It is as though, the world around her has suddenly been shut out. Within the next few minutes, she feels alright.

As this is taking place, Screenviews aren't broadcasting any new news. The authorities have had no reports on the whereabouts of the missing computers. They have announced that they have launched a widespread investigation, but have not released any details to the media, or public. It is as though, many areas of California have frozen, waiting for some significant sign that everything will be alright.

The media has made many feel unsafe and unsure, as though a destructive computer has been unleased into the world. It is, as though, there will be disastrous consequences on those who find it. Many of the stories being fabricated are saturated with talk of aliens, strange disappearances, and odd-energy fields. There are other-frightening stories that many people have already considered to be happening. There is a very heavy uneasiness stirring in the air, like an approaching-electrical storm.

On Wednesday, July 9th, it has been 13 days since Anne's strange experience. At 3:30 p.m., Anne is in a good mood and home alone. It is a beautiful day, and the sun is shining brightly throughout her home. The birds outside are chirping loudly and fluttering about. As she goes about her daily activities, she notices some strange things beginning to seize her body. She walks through the kitchen to a back room, and looks into a mirror strung on the wall. Her face is flush, and she looks at her hands and body to see if she is flush all over. Both hands are red, and she spreads her fingers apart to observe them more closely. Looking up at her face again, in the mirror, she cannot comprehend what is happening to her. She states aloud: "Huh! Maybe I'm getting sick, I must have a fever. I know, it must be my allergies, again." She walks out of the room, and continues to clean, and straightened up her home.

Soon, her husband and son will be home with hearty appetites awaiting a nice home-cooked meal. At 5:30 p.m., Anne has finished her cleaning, and heads for the kitchen to start dinner. She puts a roast in the cooktop oven, and sets the heat and energy-sensitive timer to high. It will go off only when the roast is done. While the oven heats up, the blue-blinking light regulates the temperature inside and out. It also prevents burning and overcooking. The food gently glides out to either be basted or removed. It is then automatically turned, and glides back inside. At 7:00 p.m., the light goes out, and there is a tone to indicate that the food is done. On the other side of the kitchen is a transparent-steel cooktop oven and refrigerator, which is operated by a fiber-coil plate. It works by collecting free energy, light particles and air entering onto its coil at alternating, and accelerated speeds. Heat and cold temperatures are insulated inside the oven refrigerator. It has a moisture-filter panel on the bottom, which can help foods dry out, and prevents other foods from drying out. Its' transparent-steel covering has a brown tint. There are motion dials for operation, and it never gets hot or cold to the touch. It is always at room temperature.

In this area is also where Anne prepares vegetables, and other healthy edibles, which do not take long to prepare. She also sets the self-server food preparer that takes dishes straight from the dishwasher, and onto a serving unit, where dishes are kept warm.

At 7:35 p.m., dinner is done. With the self-server set, there is not much for Anne to do, but wait until her family gets home. At a quarter-to eight the door tone sounds. While she tidies up the kitchen, the door tone sounds again. She wonders why her husband just doesn't enter, but she hurries to the door and opens it. It's her husband and son, and they have come home at the same time to surprise her. She happily greets them and says: "Hurry and get changed so we can eat. Dinner is done!" Neither of them notices her flush condition.

Bert and Bert, Jr. both head upstairs to freshen up and they both come back down together. Bert, Jr. comes downstairs and hurries to the icemaker, and fills a neon-blue colored glass with ice. Bert Sr. enters the kitchen and kisses Anne on the cheek, and pats Bert, Jr. on the shoulder.

Bert, Sr. is a quiet and gentle man with a mellow disposition. He is 45-years old with a medium build; with a slight mid-section protuberance, which he carries with pride. He walks over to the self-server to get his dinner. The plates are dropped down, and slide across a belt to a heating area, where they are warmed. Food is already placed in various compartments from the pots, and the self-server hand distributes the food onto the already-warmed plates. If need be, the plates can go back inside the self-server to be warmed over, and then served again. The numbers on the counter on the self-server shows how many people are to be served. Once it has reached this preset reading, it then shuts itself off, but keeps the food inside at a nice-warm temperature.

The family finishes eating, and the dishes are put into the full-service dishwasher, and the rest is done automatically. They sit in the living room for a few hours facing their large-bay window, which is their access to Screenview. When their enormous Screenview is not in use, it again becomes a window with a view of the entire neighborhood. It is actually built-into the window frame for watching films, shows or events. If they choose not to watch it, they can access the ScreenLink networks or simply look out the window. There is a panel inside the window, which allows access, and all of the circuits are in a transparent box that has tiny dots running through it. Each of these tiny dots works independently, and for various functions.

Angled on the coffee table is a 7"x 5" thin, transparent, curved-plastic remote panel for accessing and switching many networks and programs. On the face of the transparent panel are several-dozen tiny squares with red numbers. They are on the left side of each square, from one to 36. These squares are actually minute screens of shows playing what is currently being aired on that particular network. Networks are changed when the corresponding number or square is pressed. To get much higher networks, two or more numbers are pressed simultaneously. Programs that are from previous days, or future dates can also be viewed by selecting a panel and then selecting previous or futures. Previews are also available.

Bert Sr. shuts off the lights, and the family watches one of their favorite programs. They sit quietly in the living room. Bert Jr. sits sideways in his favorite chair, with his legs dangling over one of the chairs' arms. Anne sits in a small armchair with her elbows on the armrest, and begins to become agitated.

As she sighs and fidgets around in her chair, Bert and junior take notice. Bert asks, "What's wrong?" He then turns on the light. He notices now that her face is flush and says: "Your allergy must be acting up again, honey." She replies: "I don't feel anything. Why do you say that?" He responds: "You are as red as a beet that's why." Anne doesn't believe she's sick nor does she feel sick. Junior straightens up and stares at his mother and asks: "Dad, do you think she should go to the hospital?" Anne interrupts: "Don't be ridiculous. I'm fine! We'll watch our show and then we'll all go to bed. All I need is some rest that's all. I'll be fine in the morning you'll see." They sit together for a few hours watching Screenview before they all retire.

When Anne and Bert, Sr. enter the bedroom, she says to Bert, "I'm so tired." He yawns, and stares at her with great concern, then leans over to give her a hug. He then asks, "Can I have a kiss?" Strangely, she moves away from him, and quickly changes into a nightgown. She turns off the light, and

152

gets into bed. He asks, "What's the matter?" Anne replies: "Nothing! It's just that I'm very tired and want to get some rest." He changes into pajama bottoms, and gets into bed. He slowly moves behind her putting his arm around her waist. She rolls over and finally kisses him, and they both fall asleep.

On the morning of July 11th, Paul is again seeing into the future for the captain. The captain seems almost in a trance from all of the information pouring out at him. He asks: "What else is going to happen further into the future?" Paul hesitantly answers the question by saying, "I haven't tried to..." The captain says earnestly, "Well, let's try!"

He unabatedly demands more, and Paul knows that there is no way out, but to give the captain what he wants. Paul confesses that he does know what will happen next to Anne Welch. He becomes dumbfounded due to the captain's covetous reaction. He stops speaking, and stares quietly into space. The captain makes a physical and threatening motion with his hand and fist, as if he's about to strike.

Paul becomes angry, and his tone rises as he says: "It is as though she is right here in this building. Yes, I can see and hear what she is experiencing." The captain absorbs it all. Paul yells out: "This is enough! What do you want from me? Get me out of this place!" Paul grabs the captain by the collar, and attempts to shake him, and slam him against the wall. The captain grabs Paul's wrists, and pulls his hands from his collar. "Don't you ever put your hands on me again", he says with clenched teeth. Paul pulls back his hands and looks puzzled. He's in awe and says: "My God, you're not really physically here, and you're as light as a feather. My hands practically went through you."

The captain quietly walks to the door and gives a knock, and it's opened by one of his security staff. Paul lunges towards him, and is quickly pushed back by a large palm pushing in from outside of the door. It meets him square in the left jaw. The force is enough to knock him to the floor. He gets up again, but the door closes behind the captain. Still, he is imprisoned.

During this time, Anne Welch is at home, and begins noticing something strange happening to her body. Everything seemed to be fine all morning, but as the afternoon approaches, she knows something is just not right. She goes to her back room past the kitchen, and looks in the mirror. The sclera of her eyes and her hands are turning a very-deep red. She places her hands on her face, and notices a faint-pink glow around her fingers. Horrified, she backs away from the mirror. Too scared to run, and too scared to scream, she walks quickly to the touchpad to communicate for help.

She does not notify her family, but instead feels compelled to contact the authorities, and tells them that something is happening to her. An automated-emergency response inquires about her situation, and she shockingly states: "I think I've been exposed to something like radiation or something hot. I just don't know, I can't explain. My skin is burning-red hot; I think I'm radioactive, I have a glow. Please help me, my face and hands..."

Anne is dispatched to various agencies until reaching Captain Meyers staff, and is put on hold. She mumbles aloud: "I should tell Burt, and my son, but I can't, I..." She becomes overwhelmed with guilt, and softly begins to sob. A male voice speaks, and tells her that someone will be there shortly to help her and not to worry. Now sobbing uncontrollably, she says: "What about my husband, my son? I have to tell..." The male voice says: "It is not a good idea to have anyone else involved. You may be in a situation that may harm others, and your family. Let my people take care of you." The voice continues: "Don't worry we'll contact your family shortly." There is a short pause, and the communication ends. Anne pushes the touch pad, and just waits.

About 10-minutes later, three men arrive at her home. They've come to question her. When they enter, they are unsure as to what they see. They quickly back away from her, and leave. She cries: "No, please! Don't go! What's happening to me?" One of the men mutters, "We'll be coming back shortly." All of the men back up and then make a quick exit.

A short while later they return, but this time with transparent-protective clothing. She is escorted to a long truck, and is placed at the back in a special compartment. It is bright and surrounds her in thick glass. She sits down, and is able to talk to these three men who are midway the truck. Being dazed and confused, she is extremely upset and experiencing something terrible. One of the men tries to comfort her by saying: "You are being taken to a medical facility that will be able to help you."

As foreseen by Paul in his conversations with the captain, she is brought to the laboratory and research building. She is not far from where he is located, but on another floor. While she is brought into the building, Paul is lying back watching Screenview. Surprisingly, as he watches, he is again interrupted by the captain, but this time through the Sceenview.

Paul rises slowly, awestruck by the captain's voice filling the room. As he listens with trepidation and dread, the captain begins: "Paul all you have foreseen has come true. This has all come full circle. There you were telling me the future, and here I am telling you the future is now here. Anne Welch is here in the building."

Although Paul is taken aback, he's incensed and just stares at the Screenview. He yells out: "So what are you going to do with me now? Are you going to just keep me locked in this damn room, and use me as an Ouija board? I'd kill you if I could!" The captain continues fearlessly, and as if Paul's words have no meaning. He says: "Paul your power is priceless. I will still need you later, but right now this will be all." The captain's voice is filled with excitement that seems to demonstrate his anticipation for more information. This anticipation seems to linger in the room, long after he stops speaking, which leaves Paul in a state of mental chaos.

On Saturday, July 12th, there is no word on the whereabouts of RFactor and Eyesic. A huge investigation is still going on, and there is no trace of their disappearance.

Captain Meyers has put TC on another assignment on purpose to keep him busy, and out of the way. He constantly inquires about Paul, and the captain says, "He is taking a much-needed break. TC is highly suspicious, but is afraid to question the captain.

On this day, Paul's isolation has made him become withdrawn and depressed. It is also, on this very day that Captain Meyers enters Paul's room, with security, to speak with him. Paul is very agitated, and expresses with anger that he needs to get out. "I am done, tired, claustrophobic and going crazy," he says.

The captain smiles wryly and tells him: "Anne Welch has been taken to the detainment area." He also says solemnly: "Paul, I am going to send you home today. You have done all that is needed, and you have said all that needs to be said. I think being at home will allow you to relax, and maybe, forget about what has happened. I want you to forget what has happened, but there are just a few more things. You were right about whom and what you think I am. I've been in control of the experiment, and all of its aspects since the beginning. Sooner or later, you will learn the power and strength of my influence. I can see things long before they occur in your world. Since your race is so weak, I can see how it can be manipulated. You and your people are too easily influenced. There are many like me from the Virgo Cluster on your planet, and have been before the amazing discovery of Element G. There are others who exist in a different time continuum. We have direct links throughout your solar system.

Paul stares at him in puzzlement, and feels himself slipping more and more away from reality. He has finally gotten the truth, and it is all too real and unbelievable. He asks, "What is Element G?" The captain responds: "Unknown to you, there has been an amazing discovery in your solar system, near the planet called Saturn. What has enabled this discovery has been traveling a great distance, throughout the universe. Beings from my galaxy have been tracking your solar system for a while. Within the last year, we have been able to arrive through direct contact due to this discovery. We had to wait for human growth, awareness, and advancement to reach a certain level in order to connect and communicate. We've had various-life forms and technology readily available for someone, or something from your planet to discover. Those of us who are here are able to transcend time and space using Element G, as it is called. It creates a portal, and we can reach earth at various intervals as needed. It would take you and your people too long to travel through space conventionally. You would grow old, and we would not again have reached this moment. The scientific discovery of Element G was no accident. It was I, who made this discovery possible. It was during an interaction of an interstellar-satellite space mission crossing Saturn. I did not create Element G, but I have known of it for some time. It has been reported to have disastrous consequences, when used inappropriately in other-celestial sectors. I was able to collect samples of it from a discovery

159

from our galaxy, and create a probe that I sent through space. It was then captured during an interstellar mission near an unknown moon. The moon's discovery was also no accident either, and also uses Element G to transcend time and space. It was my ruse to allow the probe to be found at the exact same time as the appearance of this moon, and the timing was perfect. Otherwise, it would have been too obscured to be found. This element is experimental-alien genetics from many life sources. Although incredible, it is dangerous. It is a biological composition not from your world, consisting of universal blood that was removed from various-celestial sources. Also, it is a combination of other cells, and energy that can communicate. It can transcend time and space: replicate, change form and size, color, and texture. It can be used to enhance-genetic organisms and any type of device, or technology, but it can alter and destroy as well. Element G will seem like a marvel because of its incredible properties, but will be a travesty-producing biological and technological menace. It can control anything or anybody. It is not designed for human interaction, as they have not evolved enough for its use. There will be a technological war on earth. I have tested it for my own specific uses, and that is how I got here. Having your scientists believe that they have made an amazing discovery, allows us to discover how it can be used on earth. This has led us straight to you, and your scientists.

160

My people wanted to discover the effects of Element G through experimentation at our location, but decided to test it elsewhere, and discretely. We learned that it allows direct access through space. It serves as a threshold where we can come and go back and forth, when necessary. I just merely need to possess it, but this won't matter to you. While Element G continues to be utilized here by scientists, and companies for its usefulness, everyone will soon become aware of its effects. This amazing-new technology will bring about human-health advancement in various ways. Due to the anticipation of its benefits, many will be completely distracted. With its dynamic subtleness, no one will know the danger that is actually occurring. Later, I will learn the outcome of it all. This could be anything from an advanced individual, or more advanced technology. Then, I can decide if I want to experiment at my location. Hopefully, it will repeat the outcome of what happens here. It hasn't been difficult to do, as everyone is distracted with technology, and they have been for quite some time. Many have lost touch with one another and their true identity. They've lost touch with reality, and their energy flow, as well as natural surroundings. They will be unable to see the science behind the advancement. We wanted to conduct this experiment ourselves, but observed the complete dependency on technology occurring here. With all the distractions, greed, hate and betrayal, there would be no need for our intervention. No one will be aware of our presence; we have already made contact, and can monitor Element G's effects through all human interactions. Also, I was able to find a catalyst to help make this experiment possible. His name is Jim Harrison. I've been monitoring him and his intentions, and this has allowed everything to fall into place. Since you are a scientist, you may further understand what else I have to say. With Element G having all of these properties, there is something else quite interesting that I have learned about it. It redirects the energy field of anyone who comes into contact with it. Each time this technology is used by someone, an exchange of energy occurs. There will no longer be human interaction, through energy, as we know it. Eventually, energy exchange will only be possible with the help of Element G. This cellular connection will happen once someone is in contact with this technology. It will then become communicable from one person to another. Human energy is redirected towards Element G, and will be the only way one can sense another on a cellular-energy level. Most will completely rely upon this technology. They will need it to reproduce: sense, feel and react to one another. Also, this will have to be an ongoing process for continued existence. The human race will realize that this unfortunate exchange will continue for generations. It will continue until there are no longer any true-human interactions remaining. Everyone will be dealing with a new way of existence, and succumb to the challenges of interacting using this new energy.

The changes will affect everything and everyone. This includes their senses, individual organs, mentality and individuality. Unknowingly, in the beginning, this energy exchanged will occur from person to person, and only those who have not been affected will notice. Then, it will be too late. This weapon on humanity will make Element G imperative for future survival."

The captain continues: "It is you, Paul, who will be unaffected. You have been chosen to move amongst everyone else, without being noticed. I became aware early on that this technology has protected you. What I don't know is what part you will play in all of this, going forward, along with the whereabouts of the computers. I will observe the outcome of everything, as I have since the experiment began. Not to worry about Anne Welch, she is in good company with the others, who are also from the Virgo Cluster.

The captain goes on to say: "Well now, just let me also tell you about the experiment that we conducted on June 8th. The interference that occurred was from the others of my world entering into the earth's atmosphere. We were continuing the incorporation of our race into your existence. The cloning experiment was not just for testing. It was a way of letting the others know exactly what else Element G can be used for, and our exact location.

We travel on another plane of existence, but nevertheless, do catch up in your real time. We are like dust particles traveling through air particles sharing the same space and time, but constantly moving on an atomic level. I'm sorry to say Paul; there are other alien races that have found out about Element G, and our people. I'm afraid it has unwittingly led them here. This material is to them like a diamond is to you and your people. It is a very unique and highly valuable cosmic DNA. But they must be conquered, so they won't interfere."

Paul reflects back to his experience and realizes, that there truly must be an invasion of some degree occurring. Obviously, there is more than one type of alien being or beings. His thoughts are beginning to take shape. The beings that protect him are actually more spiritual and supernatural, than extraterrestrial. His connection, from his experiences, is leading him to believe in a different outcome than what the captain is telling him.

The captain continues: "I would also like for you to never, ever, mentioned any of this to anyone. Nor, admit that any of your powers ever existed."

Paul bolts up in anguish and shouts: "How could you possible ask me that? How could you think that? I'm not the only guinea pig in all of this! Everyone is going to be a guinea pig! I have to start warning…"

Paul is interrupted by several, strange-looking men that quickly enter his room. They circle the captain to protect him. The captain quietly leaves the room to never isolate, or interrogate Paul again. These men escort Paul out of his room, and to the basement of the building.

He is totally aware of his surroundings, but again, feels as if he's in a dream. While he is walking, he knows where he is going, but he cannot speak or resist his captors. Through a side door, he is lead to the underground garage to an awaiting vehicle. His vehicle is left at the laboratory, and he is taken home.

Once he arrives home and enters through the front door, he does not remember much of anything. It is as though, he has succumbed to some sort of brainwashing. He only remembers a harrowing feeling, and seeing the captain. What he does remember, clearly, is that something has happened to him. In his mind, he has interpreted this as becoming ill, and having to stay at home to recover.

In the detainment area in the building, Anne is placed in a room where she sits alone surrounded by a gray-tinted glass partition. On the other side of the partition, the captain has joined more strange-looking men who begin to question her. They appear like the ones who were with him when he was with Paul. They are very tall, lanky with an extremely-pallid complexion. Their arms are longer than they should be for their height, and very straight. Their faces are square, and their eyes are far apart and move strangely, as if they don't really see.

In many ways they act human, but they're unnerving in appearance: stiff, distant and detached. Anne is asked by one of the men about the strange events that have happened to her, and where she had been when they occurred.

The captain asks: "Have you been in one particular place for a period of time? Where were you and were you alone?" Anne nervously replies: "Well, let me think. I don't remember any instances when I was at one particular place, for a period of time, and alone. She hesitates for a moment then says: "Well, not that I haven't been alone, it's just that, I, well…" She hesitates, again, but this time she begins to have a strange recollection. "Wait, wait just a minute," she continues. "Some time ago, but I'm not quite sure, I was cooking dinner. I thought it was my husband. I thought it was his vehicle, or maybe my son, but it wasn't. When I opened the curtain to look out, I, I..." She becomes emotional, "I can't seem to remember."

As she speaks, one of the strange men behind the glass tries to comfort her as much as possible. She suddenly becomes complacent, and begins to change before their eyes. A pink glow surrounds her, with a magnificent aura that illuminates from within her body. It then fades until it disappears. The men and the captain seem baffled by this occurrence, but are not afraid.

They want her to tell her story more clearly. One of the strange men leaves the room, to go to another room, to make sure Anne is being displayed on a Screenview. As he returns, Anne has become so frightened, she is told to calm down so that she can think clearly.

Visibly shaken, Anne tries to start her story again. "When I was in the kitchen of my home, I thought I saw something outside of my window. I'm not sure at all what it could've been, but I can remember thinking it was my husband's vehicle. I don't know what happened after that, but I felt unusual, and strange. It is, as though, something had happened to me leaving me feeling this way. I just resumed my cooking and that was it." Anne's lips are quivering, as tears stream down her flush face. She is dazed and confused with a look of hopelessness. She continues: "I don't know why, I remember that part now, and nothing else.

Human men wearing protective uniforms take her from this room. Anne is placed in a radioactive and contamination-proof examination room, where she cannot harm anyone. She can be seen and heard, and observed. The captain, with the other men, witnesses all of the tests being performed on her from an adjoining room. She has psychological tests, as well as various tests for radiation exposure, and other contaminants.

Afterwards, she is proved to be of sound mind. Unfortunately, she is told that she is highly contaminated, and has massive-radiation poisoning. There is cell mutation, and an incredible metamorphous occurring within. The captain says: "Every human cell in your body has been altered. They exist in real time and space, but in a manner unknown to any of us.

The same man who had questioned her before states: "I don't know what is keeping you alive, Mrs. Welch. It is, as if, you're both dead and alive!" These words hit her hard. Sadly, she does not know that she is part of a massive-experimentation project being performed upon the human race. All of this is done by alien interaction using technology. Anne is not aware that she is the first person to become part of an alien experiment.

She has, unwittingly, become part of an experiment that is designed to help cure the maladies of the human race. This experiment, that is designed to use a simple-cloning process, has now changed course. The experiment for the betterment of everyone, on a whole, has gone wrong, terribly wrong.

It is apparent that human and alien intervention, mixed with unknown-alien substances, has caused a technological vengeance that will allow no cure. It has now turned into a different kind of malady needing a cure. In what may have been a win in the battle of diseases with a new medical treatment, may have now turned into a different type of battle.

Unknown to Anne, being surrounded by strangers in a strange place, she will never return home again. Her family is finally notified and soon after, the media is notified. Headlines all over the world have changed from the disappearance of two dangerous computers, to its first possible casualty. The incident has been labeled the beginning of a technological war. When Bert and his son receive the news of Anne's detainment, they are furious and outraged.

They were both arriving home the evening Anne was taken away, and they had no idea what had happened to her. They had called family members, neighbors, and the authorities and even scouted the surrounding neighborhoods. Unfortunately, no one remembers witnessing anything. Now that they are aware of what has taken place, they still don't know what has actually happened to her. They ask many questions, but the authorities give vague answers.

Both father and son ask angrily: "Where is she? Is she still alive? What's happening to her right now? Can we get her back? What's going on?" Bert, Sr. surmises it must be related to the media stories of the missing computers, and there must be some correlation. Suddenly, there is no further communication given to Bert Sr. Father and son will never meet Anne's captors, or know of her whereabouts, and they will be powerless to intervene.

Bert and his son have an investigation started, and are looking to capture those responsible for her disappearance. In no time, investigators enter their home probing their surroundings, and belongings. It is quarantined while being searched for clues, and evidence. Bert and his son have made living arrangements, elsewhere, for themselves until the investigation on their home is complete.

There is a Radio-Energy Magnometer placed in the kitchen and living room to scan all of the objects in the house. These dark-gray cylindrical shaped meters are made of a strange metal, and stand six-feet high. Their gray texture appears like putty or malleable clay. They also look like old-fashioned water heaters.

The outer parameter of these meters stay stationary, as the inside actually spins around like a top. There is a two-inch wide, long-white tubular bar stretching from the top to the bottom along these parameters. There is a yellow and white-fluorescent light embedded in the center of these bars. They both flash and pulsate every three seconds, as the inner part spins. A low-frequency sound is also emitted. This sound sends out energy particles, along with negative and positive light throughout the home. This energy covers all surfaces, and returns collected information and images back to the bar. All of the information is then stored in the meters.

All of this information will be analyzed and then, it will be determined, if there was a heat source of some kind. It will also determine if any of the elements in the room have altered characteristics. Any unusual objects not present to homes are checked, along with any other types of frequency.

The Magnometer's energy frequency is a specific combination: radar, sonar, x-ray, aura field and chemical analysis. It is also a particle-analysis detector, and DNA detection in one-simple unit. If anything is present, it will be made into images and shapes of the object, or residue of whatever is left behind.

Bert and his son are told by the investigators that they will need to stay out of the home for a few days, until the investigation is completed. They are both outraged; they are not only displaced, but may have lost a loved one too.

They stay with relatives, and within the next few days in their fury and grief, they think about contacting the media. They want to vent their story and predicament. Unfortunately, they do not know all of the details.

While the investigation is taking place, Anne is placed on a bed for a physical examination by a very-slender medical helper. It stands at 78-inches tall, and is neither male nor female, but takes on characteristics of both. What appears to be its head is a central-data unit. Its torso and arms function like a living being, although it is completely-mechanically created.

It is a perfectly-constructed computer capable of incredible feats. It sits on a column that works on airflow for mobility. There are no legs, but a constant-rotating movement of the columns. This propels it to the left and right, back and forth, and up and down.

As Anne sits on the bed, the medical helper lays her back. A headrest rises from the floor to the top portion of the bed. She is slowly becoming incoherent, and needs assistance to move around. Now placed in a comfortable position, the examination begins. First, a dimensional-transparent grid is placed over her face with two-dark areas that cover both eyes. The helper glides the Optiscan over her body and she is scanned.

The Optiscan is a hand-held scanner that looks like a portable showerhead with a hose. After it scans her body, it is passed over each eye while emitting an invisible light that reaches to the retina. It then takes an image of the last-powerful image that may have been burned onto her retina, and any kind of residue. If many images have been burned, the Optiscan will scan each image layer by layer. The hose attached to the Optiscan goes to a computer that develops these images onto a Screenview.

The findings are startling, and quickly displayed on the Screenview. Anne's retinas are burned in a circular pattern. It is from a powerful-energy source that leaves a grid-design pattern identical to Eyesic's lenses.

She also has a metamorphous occurring in her cells, throughout her entire body. There is a strong presence of Element G controlling her functions.

As her body transforms, it melds from human into a technological-molecular chain of communication. By containing Element G, this brings about a detectable energy connected to Eyesic and Rfactor. The captain becomes excited, and is eager to use this connection to locate the computers.

He quickly issues his staff of authority to set up energy detection, beginning within their laboratory in Las Tierras, San Diego. He has a powerful influence, and the technology to match, which will allow this type of monitoring to be possible. This detection set up will expand out towards DUG, and various cities in California.

He informs Jim Harrison of what is taking place. He states: "We may have someone here, who may have come into contact with the missing computers. She is being examined right now. I will get back to you in a moment, when her examination is finished." Jim is very excited about the news, but uses a serious tone to hide his true feelings.

The captain then orders one of the strange men accompanying him: "Have city to city surveillance towers set up. Begin immediately. We can start to monitor the whereabouts of the computers, and what is taking place. Be sure to cover these areas: Santa Monica, Long Beach, Santa Ana, and Palm Springs. Go all the way up to Redwood National Park. There is only a need for one set up in each city, and one on each end along the coastal area. Let's monitor the airspace too. Alert the media that this is taking place. It will keep them off our trail, and it will make everyone feel safe."

The captain continues: "Let's quickly set up pre-fabricated medical facilities that are free. Set them up along the same areas as the surveillance towers. We can continue experimenting with Element G in those areas. Have it available at all the facilities. Conceal it in storage units that are well insulated with layers of cement, lead, and transparent steel. We can only contain it but for so long, so we need to use it on a large scale. The storage units will work as experiments themselves. We can see what will happen in those areas, once it begins to leech out.

No one will know what is going on. They'll think the surveillance is just for monitoring the missing computers, and anything that may be occurring. It will calm their fears and make this run smoothly. Have MCR's in each facility and Screenviews in window display offering all of the treatment options available to everyone. Make the facilities very welcoming and friendly; whereas, anyone can walk in regardless of having any benefits. It will make those who are curious about the free services want to volunteer for treatment. There are a lot of sick people who would like to receive free-medical treatment of some kind or another. We can then monitor the effects, so we need to begin as soon as possible."

As the examination ends, Anne is kept in a special room behind tinted glass. She is covered in a bright-pink glow. It hurts an unaided eye to look at her in this state. She now has to be monitored by computers and helpers. Those in charge, who are seeing her through the glass cannot and will not do anything for her. They are just waiting to see her outcome.

The captain, again, contacts Jim and states: "The woman I mentioned to you is named Anne Welch. She was brought into the laboratory on her own cognizance, because she thinks something unexplainable has happened to her." He goes on to describe the specifics with all of the details of what has taken place. He says: "Since she has been here, she has been examined. Anne has now quickly turned into a halo of glowing-red light energy." Jim is stunned and can barely contain himself.

The captain continues: "She no longer resembles anything that could have once proved she was a woman or human. The helper can no longer provide any assistance to her, and what is left will be kept under observation. As Element G was detected in her, it has left a trail that we will be monitoring from the set up in California. This will help determine the outcome of all of this. I want you to be the contact at DUG to arrange all of this on your end. I will explain more of it later. Right now, I will tell you this: "Anne lived with her husband, Bert Welch and son on the outskirts of the laboratory in Las Tierras. They have been notified that she was taken away. They know nothing of her whereabouts or what is happening to her, and I would like to keep it that way."

Jim is trying to digest all of the information he has just received, and thinks it is all too easy. After speaking with the captain, he immediately sets about trying to find Bert and his son using his connections.

On July 16th, the investigation on Bert Welch's home is complete, and the findings are startling. The entire home is covered with radiation, and strange energy particles. A lot of the characteristics of the home have changed, and the infrastructure has been altered. It seems that it will be unable to support itself over time. The kitchen has the most damage, and there are visible signs of cracks and scorching. There is a reddish-grid pattern burned onto one of the walls, near the appliances.

Bert and his son cannot return home. Their investigator arranges temporary housing for them near their relatives, a few towns away. They are told that their home has been contaminated, and they will be provided for indefinitely.

They are both unhappy with the entire situation, and orchestrate how to vent their frustrations. Reluctantly, they move into their sparsely furnished, and simple, two-bedroom apartment.

Not soon after they arrive, Jim Harrison is able to locate them, and speaks to them through their new home's touchpad. He explains to them what has happened to Anne. Bert Sr. is so overwrought; he can barely listen to what he's hearing. Jim identifies himself as an informant, as to remain anonymous. He proceeds with caution to make himself appear innocent of the whole situation. He reiterates everything that the captain has told him about Anne. Unfortunately, it is not out of concern that he shares this information, but in hopes of fueling his revenge.

Bert Sr. then contacts the media with this information, and a frenzy of fear and panic quickly spread. From Screenviews to people on the street, everyone is talking about the missing computers and Anne Welch. The media describes how Anne has been examined, and is being kept in a special room behind tinted glass. It also states that she has become a genetic-cellular mutation of some kind, and is covered in a bright-pink glow.

Her family and friends are all shocked, baffled and afraid. They are hoping for some miracle that she is contacted and found alive and alright.

CHAPTER 7

Several days later, on the evening of July 23rd, a young girl named Tanya is taken to Memorial Hospital of Laboratory Science in California. She is taken there along with her uncle Carlton Coppola, nicknamed Cab.

As Tanya recounts an incident that they both encountered, she tells the hospital staff and the authorities an incredible story. She terrifying states: "My uncle and I were alone, on a dark and winding road in Santa Barbara. As Uncle Cab was driving, we saw two, bright-pink shimmering lights in the distance. It was on the road in front of us. He tried to get closer to look at what was in the distance. We both looked to the left, and to the right of the lights trying to figure out what it could be. We looked all around. He slowed down, but the lights kept coming until they got very close. So then, he came to a complete stop, and the lights stopped too. We didn't move for a long time, until the lights started to move. Then they began to move, again, very slowly."

She becomes hysterical and sobs: "Then, it was there in front of us. It was surrounded by a very-deep pink color. My uncle was so scared, he tried to turn around. He stepped on the gas pedal by mistake, and went forward into the lights. There was this big flash of reddish-pink light. When he stopped, we

180

both got out of the vehicle and ran. I was running so fast, I was ahead of my uncle, and I couldn't see him. Then there was another bright-pink flash, and I just remember being on my knees on the ground. It was hot and damp. When I got up, the vehicle was shining. It was smoking like it was burning. There was light in it, or something neon. I could see through it." Tanya sobs, "But I didn't see Cab." She continues: "There was something dark on the ground. Then, these strange authority people came, and a strange ambulance. They wouldn't let me go near the vehicle to find my uncle. I had to ride in a vehicle with medical people, who never spoke to me."

Tanya's family is contacted, and she is treated for shock, and released from the hospital. Cab is pronounced dead and unrecognizable on arrival. Later, his charred remains and vehicle are spirited away by scientists. It is then given to the captain's personal authority for investigation. Tanya and her family are told that an investigation is underway, and they will be informed when it is completed.

In Captain Meyer's office, within the laboratory building, he receives information from Coroner, Bill Keith. As Bill determines Cab Cappola's cause of death, the captain discusses some of the incident regarding Anne Welch. His information stuns the coroner, as this is something beyond his scope of medicine. As Bill listens, he knows that the conversation they're having is to be kept strictly confidential, to the highest level. The unbelievable details put Bill in a very precarious situation. His limited knowledge on this matter may jeopardize his health and career.

As the captain continues, the coroner has no choice but to agree, and do as instructed. His is apprehensive and fearful, feeling pressured by the captain's authority. He wants to ask questions, as to those involved with the incident. Realizing this is a matter dealing with top officials, he decides to just go along with it. He listens and only says calmly, "Yes sir. That's right, Captain Meyers. I think what you're describing about Mrs. Welch is possibly what may have happened to Mr. Cappola."

Bill continues: "It seems that Mr. Coppola was attacked by something. The report says, 'He was lying on the road when he has found.' " Bill says, "Some authority personnel named Mr. Francis Tipp said that Mr. Coppola was aglow in some sort of pink light. Mr. Tipp described that when he got closer to the body, he didn't seem to know what Mr. Coppola was. Before the body was admitted to the hospital, it was covered in a blanket. It was injected with some sort of a solution." Bill stops reading the report and states inquisitively, "Some unknown authorities must have intervened." He continues reading the report: 'The blanket that covered the body was a lightweight-repelling material. It stopped the glow from emanating from beyond the body.' " Bill, comments: "He was long dead before he got to the hospital." He finishes reading the report, "Mr. Tipp's stated: 'Mr. Coppola's pink color was throughout his body. It then faded until disappearing completely. There were trails of smoke coming from various parts of his body.' "

The captain instructs Bill to remain silent on his findings, and the entire incident. The coroner says: "From the way I hear it captain, the authorities or whoever are responsible for all of this are pretty hush, hush. The media says the incident has been deemed Top Secret."

Unfortunately, the coroner does not know that he, too, is now a part of this terrifying and devastating ruse. The captain, who knows all, is not saying a word. He is just letting the coroner speak. The captain finally says: "Speaking of the media, I will have a statement issued at once. Stay in touch, and keep me abreast of any new developments." Their conversation ends.

The same news travels worldwide. No one has yet been able to explain the disappearance of the computers, or its unconfirmed victims. It is being called a phenomenon that has sparked a world-wide search by various agencies. The media is calling for an "On the Alert Status" to be declared throughout the world.

The captain's intent is to quiet all of the angry outbursts, and quell the rampant rumors from the panic-stricken populous. His media-relations personnel issues a public statement to the world, that the computers have not been found. Also mentioned, is that the authorities are working 24-hours a day, seven-days a week, and they're using every resource available to locate them. The public is made aware that they are in no-present danger, and the incident that occurred was due to an unfortunate-scientific mishap.

The captain's true concern is the outcome of the experiment, and not locating the computers. He wants to bide his time to find out the effects of Element G on a large scale. As he pretends to search for the computers, this allows him to continuously monitor each incident.

On Friday, July 25th, at 1:00 p.m., at The Hospital of Laboratory Science in Santa Barbara, Captain Meyers has a special-morgue unit set up. The unit is located in the basement, and is a cube within an existing room. The door to the unit is the only access in and out, and for entering the outer-surrounding room. A secret autopsy will be performed on the remains of Cab Coppola. The coroner, Bill Keith is assigned to the location on orders by the captain. He is apprehensive, while contemplating what he is about to do. He has never performed an autopsy on anything like this before.

In this bright-white streamlined, state-of-the art unit, the technology is incredibly advanced. A few decades earlier, it would take more than three rooms to equal the capacity that is compacted within this space. There is a medical helper, Screenview monitors, and various-technical equipment. It has transparent-steel surgical equipment for precision, as well as magnetic devices for the medical helper to use. It is a gloveless facility, and has a vacuum-waste flow system; which makes the unit time and cost effective. Hands never have to come into contact with germs, chemicals or fluids.

Bill looks at Cab's remains, as if there is something familiar about them, as if the remains could speak. Using the equipment, he then begins to work. After about 20 minutes, he notices something happening with the overhead lights. He pauses, and then looks up. The lights seem to be functioning properly. Then, they begin to flicker and, again, function properly.

Bill is thinking that it's just a power issue, and he continues to work. This time the lights flicker, and go off. Agitated, he walks towards the wall, and rubs his palm against the units hanging-light panel. The lights come back on again. For a brief moment, they seem to be all right.

He walks back to the remains, and the lights flicker again. This time it's quicker, and they begin to dim, as if losing power. Bill is becoming quite uneasy, as the lights begin to turn pink. He is now becoming terrified, and doesn't know what to do. He backs up against a tray, and some of his equipment falls to the floor making a loud-crashing sound. The medical helper is motionless, as if affected by an energy drain.

Bill can't decide whether to stay in the room or run out. In the dimness, he becomes frozen with fright. In a desperate last-minute effort, he walks over again to the light panel. He wipes his palm across it, but nothing happens.

With minimum visibility, he runs back to the other side of the unit. Just as he does, the lights briefly come back on. His attention is caught by some significant changes in Cab Coppola's remains. Terrified and dumbfounded, he just stares hypnotically in silence. The remains are taking on the same-pink glow as it had before, and energized crystals begin surrounding it.

As he rushes out of the unit, he runs down a narrow hall slamming right into Captain Meyers. He is terrified and says: "The body is beginning to glow for some reason." The captain begins to answer, but Bill does not let him speak. Bill can barely talk now from fear, and rambles, "The lights are changing. Something strange is going on. Are those computers in this area, or are they with you? I don't know what could be causing this. Where are those computers? Can they do this?" The captain hears Bill's panic and reassures him, "Your imagination has caused your hysteria." Bill shouts back: "Hysterical? Do you think I'm hysterical? I'm not hysterical! This is something that I have never seen before that is happening in that unit. I think you need to bring your authority people here so everyone can see for themselves."

A short time later, the captain's authority personnel arrive at the unit along with TC, who has been briefed by the captain. Other scientists and analysts arrive, and they all join the captain. TC is with a couple of his staff members. They are carrying universal-recording equipment: heat and light-sensitive devices, specialized-lightweight HSD's, and radiation equipment. While those in the unit stare upon the remains of a charred body, they all have a look of astonishment across their faces.

Cab's remains have a constant-pink glow surrounding it. Suddenly, the unit becomes bright with light, then quickly extinguishes, leaving everyone at a standstill. There are sounds of gasps heard from everyone in the unit being suddenly thrust into darkness. The only other light source comes from natural light. It is from dim-light filtering through a window on the left side of the room. It is high up above the unit, near the corner, and close to the ceiling. It is magnetically controlled, and covered in a dirty film of dust. This is attributed to static electricity, and having never been cleaned.

There is only one other sound heard, accompanying the gasps. It is from the low and steady hum of the built-in solar powered air-conditioning system.

As their eyes adjust in the dark, the light from the window now seems quite bright in contrast to the unlit unit. The small-rectangular widow faces a gray, walled-in side of its adjoining building. There is a dead end in between these two spaces. A narrow and cracked-concrete walkway runs in between these two spaces. Bright-sunlight shines down upon the walkway drenching the entire space with white light. The walkway goes all the way out onto street level. The view does not allow much more, than to see a tiny-ant crawling around on a blade of grass. In comparison to a little ant, the blade-of-grass seems as tall as a tree.

As they stand around stunned, waiting for the captain to take control of the situation, they can faintly see each other's faces. One of TC's staff members feels for the light panel to turn the lights back on. When the lights do come back on, they are very dim, and just barely enough to adequately light the room.

Suddenly, on the wall behind Cab's remains, appears a small, dark-round void. It is actually an opening with frayed and faded edges. It grows larger and slowly spreads outwards along the unit until it reaches a terrifying diameter of six feet. The opening is pitch-black, and it leads straight into an area that seems to be of some other plane of existence. It clearly appears like a sinkhole in the wall.

Everyone backs up simultaneously, and no one speaks. They are unprepared for what they see, and do not know what they are about to undertake. It is a terrifying and unsettling sight. They are looking into an opening that now has something moving within. There is no light and a frightfully, strange sound can be heard. It sounds like air rushing in, and being gulped into a hole. It is impossible to tell which direction the opening travels, as it is so black and seems without end.

The captain suspiciously bends down and looks under the table. He sees that the void extends all the way to the floor, and some of the floor has disappeared. The strange-suction sound is actually the floor, walls and ceiling dissolving very slowly, and seeping in. This has everyone stopped in their tracks, as they fear being sucked into this abyss. Although this is happening, somehow, there is no structural change in the unit.

As the captain slowly rises back up, he looks upon the remains on the table. Along with everyone else, he sees energized crystals coming from the remains spiraling into the void. It appears it's claiming something from the remains. Just then, a glowing-white outline of something appears in the void that is covering over something black. It is not human, but it is alive with energy crystals similar to Element G. It resembles the being that Paul DeAngelo experienced. As it gets closer, it gets brighter. On various areas on this strange being, pin points of light seep through. It seems to be carrying something. When it gets close to the opening of the void, it stops and begins to speak.

As the voice of the strange form speaks, it seems to be staring at everyone in the unit. The voice is calm, but firm and matter of fact. The tone is directive: "This energy that I carry is trapped, and tangled in a dimensional state. It is suspended technologically and genetically." Everyone in the room is tongue tied, and cannot mutter a sound. It appears as if it is holding Cab's energy in some unknown form, as the remains still lie on the table.

The being continues: "Where I am standing, an energy shift has begun. It is also at another-nearby location. A technological development mixed with energy created this interference and transference. It has caused things to traverse where they do not belong. What I am holding, is part of what is laying there in front of all of you. It contains genetic material that is not from this area in time and space. It connects to the existence of where I and many others come from. My location is within the Andromeda Galaxy, and the others are along the Milky Way. This material was developed by many-universal races on various levels. It is for travel, communication, and genomic development of certain species and life forms. This material is kept, and housed by many in the universe. It has the ability to move about on its own. It is usually secured, and used in exploration missions. Many know how to use it, and it is continuously evolving. This material is made up of many cells, and some have been added during research. Some have been collected, and incorporated while traveling on scheduled journeys throughout space. Each cell consists of alien plasma, neurons, and radioactive particles. There is also an anti-gravitation system, an energy field, and various reproductive-life forms. It was developed to open space for distance using this collected-universal energy. This creates a chain of energy traversing through space, reaching other cells, connecting and collecting at a source. These incredibly powerful cells traverse through space going out in various directions. They can go in and out of each other, and are in and of its self. They are each independent, and operate on a whole and can reproduce to adapt to their environment. They move energy, substances, and matter once making contact. This also allows for a short duration of travel time, through long distances in space. It was created for this purpose only. Some of these cells have been taken during a mission, and are being used here. Their potential benefits have already begun creating disastrous events. There will be consequences for possessing it, creating unstoppable and totally irreversible chaos. As these cells make it very easy to go from one place to another, mixing them has caused a paradox. There are separations of places and spaces, rips and alterations, as technology interrupts these energies. Many aliens may come to recover this material. All of it must be collected, and then this will end. If the material can be released into the atmosphere, it will go back into interstellar space. The remains on the table contain this alien material, but have since become its victim. It had been genetically altered before it was destroyed, and the deadly outcome was due to the technological mixture. The effect on living organisms will be different than the effect on non-living organisms. These remains will be proof of what is the beginning, and will continue to proliferate, unabatedly. There is a man who works at a secret-underground location, who is using this powerful material. He wants to develop it for destructive purposes. He is a fortuitous-white male, forty-one years old, and five-foot nine. He has a slender build, dirty-blonde hair, and a wide nose. He has a thick-bushy mustache, and there are signs on his face showing he suffered acne. He has let his hair grow to his shoulders, and keeps it tied behind his head. Finding his secret location may be helpful in finding him. Look for a white-wash office building in San Diego, with an orange and purple chevron, on the far side. This logo is DUG's symbol that only someone on the inside would know. This must be done quickly or no one will be able to fight back. Everyone will become exposed to the same technological-genetic makeup. They will not be able to help one another, even if they survive. It will affect many, and many will readily volunteer for experiments using this material. There will be no way out from this outcome. Many will be deceived into thinking it's a cure for various things. It has to be stopped immediately or it will, decidedly, be the beginning of an alien-technological war."

The being, then appears to turn and stare deliberately, and directly at the captain. It says: "I know who, and what you are. You are from the Virgo Cluster, and are one of the beings here helping to cause destruction by using this material." The eyes of everyone in the unit are now upon the captain. The being then says: "You are like the ones, who I have seen here, on this side of the universe. This opening is your entry of how you arrived here, and your means of transport!"

The being then warns everyone else in the room: "He is not human, and is experimenting with this material on a terrible mission. He has been experimenting on various people, and objects through the use of cloning, with a deceitful purpose. No one has been made aware, as to what is really going on."

All of the shadowed faces in the room stare frightfully, and in disbelief at the captain. Now that the captain's true identity is known, he tries to break away. Just then, the being begins to disappear, and that strange sound of rushing air returns in the void. Everyone is briefly distracted by this occurrence, except for the captain. He motions to his men of an escape. Before they charge out of the room, the captain decides to get rid of the evidence. He quickly pushes the table with Cab's remains into the void, and it disappears into the blackness. The coroner yells, "What are you doing?"

Mostly everyone in the unit is shouting in horror at this unbelievable action. Suddenly, the void begins to shrink. It fades until disappearing, as the solid wall returns. The room again fills with light, and the captain and his men are already out the door. One of TC's men tries to catch the last man before he exits. As others also try to help, someone trips on some fallen equipment creating an obstacle for all. This allows the captain and his men to close the door, and lock it before anyone reaches them.

The coroner is able to open the door. As he and the others run out, they are met with a dreadful obstacle. There is another large-black void on the floor that appears like a sinkhole. As it quickly closes, it appears to be pulling the floor and walls within. Everyone rushes back to the unit. A few seconds later, TC looks out the door. He notices the floor is intact, but the captain and his men are nowhere to be found. They all surmise that he escaped with his men through the void.

TC exclaims: "The captain has to be stopped! He has planned a devastating attack on this planet, and has already set the wheels in motion." TC cannot believe the words actually uttered out of his own mouth. He looks surprised, but continues his stance. He instructs his staff to go to the media, and to other authorities: "Alert the scientific community of what has just happened."

The captain secretly appears at DUG through the same threshold, from where he had disappeared from the morgue. There he meets up with Jim Harrison, who is working in his laboratory. Jim is surprised to see the captain. Before the captain can speak, he receives communication through his wafer implant. One of his personnel says to him: "What remained of Anne Welch has disappeared from the laboratory and not in the same manner as we travel. There was no opening, and she simply dematerialized. The computers have also been detected by the surveillance, but have not actually been seen. There has been some random chatter in various neighborhoods in San Diego and Santa Monica. Some civilians have reported seeing pink bands of light at night. These lights have been appearing, and disappearing around buildings, and homes. Right now many seem concerned. No fatalities or major incidences have been reported, but something is starting to stir."

The captain contemplates what he may have started, and what it may mean for him. He ends the communication. He now focuses on the look of curiosity written all over Jim's face. He says to him: "Anne Welch has disappeared. I am not sure what this means at the moment. We have to discuss something very important that needs to be done." The captain is harried. As he begins to explain the situation, Jim is more than happy, willing, and able to assist.

He half-truthfully begins to explain: "Jim, I need your help! I need for you to do something, but first, I am going to briefly explain Element G. It is really a laboratory-created chemical molecule designed to function as a binding agent. It is only supposed to be used in this way. It is used medically to alter specific-human cells that have mutated. It has become a concern that it may have gotten into the wrong hands." Jim raises his brows and his eyes widen. The captain continues: "This knowledge will only be shared between the two of us." Jim nods his head in acknowledgment, but as always he's in constant pursuit of revenge, and victory.

He then orders Jim to a task: "Collect all of Element G here in the laboratory. We will need to take it to a secret location next week." Jim is more than happy to oblige. He does not realize that the captain is lying to him to cover his tracks. The captain continues: "I have been informed that Element G may get stolen, and it may be by those who stole the computers. We need to protect it."

Jim's thoughts interpret this as giving him more leverage in his goal. He can now place blame on the captain, and Harve Ryan as a result of Element G. He's also, thinking: "Why should I deliver all of Element G into the captain's hands? What if it turns out to be beneficial? I'll keep some here in my laboratory just in case. If it comes down to it, I can say it was with the captain all along, and I wanted to keep it as evidence. I'll be the hero for bringing in the bad guys."

The captain says: "Let me show you where all of Element G is housed here at DUG. Over the weekend you will have time to gather it all, and we can meet again next week. Jim asks, "Where will that be?" The captain responds: "We'll meet at The Laboratory and Research Organization building. I will supply you with a clearance, and you will have no problem entering the laboratory."

All the while, the captain has not led Jim on to his true identity. While Jim is blinded by his greed, he does not know that the captain is using him.

CHAPTER 8

On Monday, July 28th at 8:30 a.m., the captain and Jim Harrison and a couple of DUG's crew workers meet. They quietly and secretly appear at the laboratory. They are rolling in a few-concealed packages, covered in concrete and transparent steel containing Element G. They enter through the garage, and head towards the large elevator and ascend to the eighth-floor storage area.

After they unload all of the packages, the captain says to Jim: "You and the crew go out ahead of me. I'll finish here." The captain wants to put some distance been himself and the others, in case they are caught. The distance will allow him more time to escape. At 8:57 a.m., Jim and the crew enter the elevator, and it stops on the 7th floor. A member of TC's staff enters, and he recognizes Jim from the description, given by the apparition at the morgue. He doesn't say anything, but afterwards, he quickly reports it to TC.

TC immediately contacts a special authority, who head to the laboratory in search of Jim, and the captain. A warrant is issued for both of their arrests. The authorities waste no time getting to the laboratory, and arrive within six minutes. Jim has already gone, but they head up to the 8th floor, and find the captain still there. Two uniformed-authority personnel try to apprehend him. He vanishes in a large-black void in a corner carrying a portion of Element G.

They are taken aback by this bizarre occurrence, and freeze in their tracks. There are sealed packages on the floor, and neither risk getting close to them, not knowing what they may contain inside. A security helper is summoned that immediately, removes the packages to a private room in the laboratory.

The authorities suspect that the captain uses this material in the packages to keep him from any harm. They believe it allows him to, eerily, transport safely from place to place. Unable to capture Jim or the captain, they are now deemed as fugitives and dangerous men. A warrant is issued within the scientific community for their capture.

Over the next few weeks, there is no sign of Jim or the captain. The captain has taken refuge at a private dwelling, at an undisclosed location on the outskirts of Las Tierras. From this location, he secretly continues communicating with his organizers who are building the medical facilities. He states to them: "Begin recruiting some of our people from DUG to the San Diego location, who have training using the MCR's and Screenviews. The others can go to the other locations."

The remainder of July, through the entire month of August, brings to fruition his request of pre-fabricated medical establishments. In this short period of time, the organized workers starting in San Diego have already progressed along the West Coast. Having quickly spread across state lines, they are already in major cities on the East Coast.

Each facility offers individuals a small, but amazingly comfortable, and private section that appears like a room in their own home. The sections are completely open to everyone's view when entering. When patients enter their section, they are amazed to find that it is unseen by all of those around them. It is also sound proof. Unknown to everyone passing through, all sections are totally surrounded by a wall that uses the same principles of Screenview. In contrast to this inviting environment, it has a slight and austere clinical-care setting.

On August 22nd, the San Diego location is opened to the public. A window Screenview displays that it is receiving new patients, and what is being offered. The display disclaimer states: "This is a new and innovative 24-hour clinical care facility that accepts appointments, and walk-ins. There is no long-wait time, and all are welcome regardless of race, age, health condition, or financial status. We offer one-hundred percent complete privacy to all, and no physical examination is required. This is a safe, pain-free and worry-free establishment. There are no medicines, chemicals, or injections. There are also no vaccines or surgery. This facility is designed to cure illnesses ranging from communicable-social diseases to cancer. It is cost free, and provides a quick and effective treatment for illnesses. It is the hope of this facility to eradicate diseases that previously had no cures. It is completely regulated, and sustained by the governing authorities of health. Please note: All cures from previous patients and participants will be given to other patients for cures upon request. This procedure is especially helpful and recommended and is designed for children seeking quick treatments. Volunteers are welcome!" At the bottom it states: "There are no side effects."

Throughout the day, many walk by and inquire, and others are not sure. Some decide to make an appointment for another time. That evening at 9:45 p.m., a couple is out on a stroll. They are discussing medical concerns, and are the first patients that actually enter seeking treatment. They are New Americans, Tammy and Harry both 35-years old, and in a long-term relationship. Tammy has breast cancer, and is seeking a quick and safe-alternative treatment. She is immediately struck by the unique façade, and the friendly and welcoming environment. She feels this may be the place she has been looking for.

They are greeted by a beautiful-young woman. She is a red head with a perfect-olive complexion. She is a DUG worker, and from the Virgo Cluster. She says, "Hi, my name is Greta. Welcome to the facility!" Tammy smiles, and glances around and notices the openness. She inquires about the lack of privacy. Greta assures her: "When I show you to your section, you will see that it is completely private." Tammy looks at Harry for his approval. He raises his brows, and with a tight-lipped smile shrugs his shoulders. Greta assures them both what is to take place. They become more at ease, as she takes Tammy to a section.

Harry, hesitatingly, sits in a nicely-furnished waiting area, and watches Screenview. As Tammy enters her section, she momentarily looks over her shoulder at her boyfriend. She becomes frightened, as she cannot see the waiting area that she has just passed. She cannot figure out why she is surrounding by a crystal wall, and can only see within her section. Greta explains: "It the latest in advancement within these new, one-of-a kind medical facilities.

Tammy presents her UIS card, and all of her personal and medical information appears in a matter of seconds. It is directly displayed on the Screenview in her section. All of the information needed is provided, and no other physical information is exchanged. The process is complete.

203

Greta says to her: "Tammy you can undress, and cover with this. I will be right here, as the room darkens for your privacy." It is a sheet, and it is see through appearing like Chiffon. Tammy looks at her in disbelief, and again, Greta addresses her concerns. She says: "Don't worry, it is very comfortable, and will cover and conceal you completely."

As the lights dim, Tammy undresses. A medical helper comes out of a corner that had been previously motionless before. She is startled, and unsettled, as the helper takes her clothing. She, hesitantly, lays nude under the sheet, on a beautiful bed.

The translucent helper is divided into three sections that are connected by transparent steel. It is here, within the connected sections where it gets its power. It has a cylindrical opening at the top section surrounded by a gray border, which is its visual area. Its two limbs on either side extend, and retract when necessary. Its movements are delicate and smooth, but it is massively strong and agile. It glides across the floor on airflow.

The helper touches the sheet, and instantly the sheet adheres and conforms to the shape of Tammy's breasts. It then spreads out gently, to cover the rest of her body, from the shoulders to her feet. She calls out in fear from within the dark. Greta comforts her: "Don't be afraid, this is my helper Tabita. She assists me along with collecting your belongings, until the treatment is completed. According to the area being treated, the sheet is programmed to adhere to it, and where you are having symptoms. Neither I, nor Tabita can see through it."

The section's lights come back on, and Greta smiles, and softly pats Tammy's shoulder. She asks: "Are you okay now, are you comfortable?" Tammy replies: "Yes, but this is so new to me." Greta explains: "You have absolutely nothing to fear, and you can see everything as it is taking place.

Tabita slides open a drawer to a cabinet next to the bed. She pulls out a MCR, and gives it to Greta and turns towards the Screenview. Greta stands over the bed, and explains the process to Tammy step by step. As she begins to move it over Tammy's breast, the particles in the MCR move around rapidly. It extracts the diseased and healthy cells that instantly appear on the Screenview. Tabita prepares a blue dye in a shallow dish containing Element G, and shines light-energy vibrations onto it. Greta moves the MCR over the dish, while invisibly extracting the solution that stick to the already extracted cells. The process is shown on Screenview. It is an amazing sight, as the diseased portion of the cell has turned bright blue. The microantibodies immediately surround the healthy cells and the process repeats to all surrounding cells.

Greta moves the MCR back over Tammy's breasts again with the treated cells. They immediately begin cloning within Tammy, displaying it on the Screenview. As the cancer is instantly being recognized and eliminated, the light energy goes throughout her body. It is alerting other cells of the oncoming treatment. Tabita readies another container for holding, and saving some of the treated cells in the MCR to give to other patients.

Greta tells Tammy to get dressed, as the lights dim. Tabita brings her clothes, and belongings back to her. The sheet releases her, and she feels fantastic. She is amazed, and shocked at the same time knowing that her body has already begun to heal itself.

Almost immediately, she begins to feel an incredible sensation throughout her body. She does not share it with the Greta, or the medical helper. At 10:00 p.m., she leaves the section, and meets her boyfriend in the waiting area. He exclaims, "Wow that was fast!" She gives him a flirtatious smile, and he wonders what has taken place. She says, "Let's go," and they leave the facility.

When they get outside she says to him: "I feel strange, aroused in a strange sort of way. I can't explain it." He asks, "You mean like aroused like...?" She responds: "Yes, but not really like a real one, but like a pseudo-sexual orgasm or something. Let's get out of here, and I'll explain it more." Their conversation is in earshot of another couple not too far behind, who have been drinking heavily.

The inebriated couple looks at the facility, and immediately gets the wrong idea. They read the disclaimer, and in their current state decide to volunteer. They have their healthy cells cloned, and unwittingly exposed themselves to Element G.

Once the couple have finished, they leave and begin to experience the same sensations as Tammy. Somehow, they have become sober and suddenly realize what they may have done. They're exciting by what they're experiencing, as they believe was an intimate encounter. They laugh about it, and immediately tell their friends.

Within the last week of August, Tammy and Harry are suddenly drifting apart. He blames her latest medical treatment, on her distancing herself from him.

Many others have visited the facilities through word-of-mouth. Others volunteer to experience the amazing-side effects. Some have found dramatic changes in their health, and personality changes in others. Quite a few are exhibiting signs of heightened awareness. There are those who feel their health deteriorating, and are unable to relate with normal-human reactions.

More facilities open nationwide. Many visit these locations, and begin to have the same experiences. Happily for the captain, everything is going along as planned.

Some that are lulled in to volunteer, with a low tolerance to the treatment, experience the side effects right away. They are alarmed, but are afraid to discuss it with their technicians. They, also, immediately tell their friends and acquaintances and the information continues to spread rapidly. Also, those who've had healthy relationships prior to the experiment are finding, they are losing connections to their partners.

As the news of this treatment continues to spread, many welcome it as a relief. Since they have been so consumed by years of various-other forms of technological stimulation, this offers an acceptable and enjoyable form of interaction. Those who are tired of distant relationships, and an almost-forgotten family unit, conspire. This makes people volunteer by the dozens, as they feel they are doing something worthwhile.

Unbeknownst to all, their lives will be changed forever. The entire process seems harmless at first, until they realize the reproductive and genetic implications of the experiment.

Within this time, many more have entered these state-wide facilities appearing everywhere. What they are finding are similar experiences and symptoms. Odd occurrences are also happening, as things change and break down around them.

Something is occurring on a not-so-busy street on Dyver Avenue in Los Angeles. In a section near Inglewood, a woman and her young son are going to a tech bank. This is for a simple-credit transaction. They use the outside Screenview kiosk, and the woman holds up her UIS card. Her credit transaction is complete. Suddenly, as she pulls the card away to watch the display on the screen, there is nothing legible that she can understand. The writing looks scrambled like hieroglyphics.

She again shows her card, as the writing begins to behave strangely. Along with her son, they cautiously take small steps backwards. The message being displayed reads, "Error, this account has been closed. All information on this account has been deactivate, and deleted." The frightened woman rereads the message, and cannot understand what is happening. Another message is displayed that flashes, "Deactivated."

They go inside the tech bank to talk with an automated-Screenview helper, in regards to her recent transaction. While displaying her card she states: "My card has been deactivated, and I don't know why. I want it reactivated." The helper replies: "That card is not in the universal system, and the user does not exist." The woman voice exalts, "What do you mean does not exist? I've had this card forever, and all of my information is on it. How can I get another card? Maybe my information has been stolen. How do I report it?" The helper replies: "It is not stolen, there is no information of any kind on this account, and there is no history. There is nothing in the data banks."

The woman knows the entire UIS system includes everything, and is connected to one source. In fear and in disbelief the woman blurts out: "So this means, I don't exist? What am I supposed to do? I have a family, and all of my information is gone. How am I supposed to survive?" The helper says: "I am sorry, but there is no such account in the data banks." The helper shuts down, and there is no more communication. The woman tearfully grabs her son, and very abruptly bursts open the door with a crash. They hurry out to the street towards a grocery outlet.

She picks up a couple of items, and again, uses her UIS card to check herself out. The information displays that the card is inactive. Leaving her items on the side of the counter, and not wanting to draw any attention, they quietly walk out. She has never known of any UIS card holder to be deactivated, and not in the system. At a loss as to what to do, they head home.

Many people in several cities have slowly begun to feel, and notice the effects of the technological change. These strange occurrences are first noticed in California: The Mid-West, South West, and are spreading. Reports are coming from areas along the South East Atlantic Coast, and the East Coast. Some are unsure of what is taking place, while others fear for their safety.

The captain's influence is spreading worldwide. More pre-fabricated facilities are slated to appear in the coming months to include Europe. One particular area is next to the Culverton Housing Development, in a section of Carlisle in the United Kingdom.

Little-by-little UIS cardholders are losing their identities. They are removed from the universal system without any explanation, and can no longer interact with the remaining-identified citizens. As they, unfortunately, physically no longer exist in the system, many of them begin to bunk up together with families. This strange-technological elimination randomly selects certain family members leaving them without identity. They have no choice but to rely upon others. Those who do not have families or partners, but who remain in the system are forced to take drastic measures. They try to survive by protecting themselves. There are many families, who have begun to send those who are eliminated away. Many, who have not been eliminated, have become panicked. They believe that the others will turn against them, to take all of their possessions.

On August 29th, at 1:17 p.m., a media announcement has been scheduled. A special emergency report is about to be issued. A woman reporter begins announcing: "This is a special report from the Screenview Media Network. Just a few moments ago, reports have been coming in about many people becoming ill. This is after receiving treatments at the new-medical facilities, throughout the state of California, and various other cities. There are also reports about strange-identity thefts, and people losing access to their information. There are disturbing occurrences within their surroundings and disturbances to others who they are in contact with…" Before she finishes her sentence, there is a strange rumbling sound heard. It is within the large-news studio, and it is coming from the floor. It grabs her attention, as well as all the crew and technicians.

In the center of the studio, the floor appears to warp inwards. There is a loud sound, as if air is rushing through a tunnel. As everyone backs away from the area, the floor buckles. It is as if being pulled down from below, and swallowed into a void. The area becomes a black sinkhole. Although this is happening, nothing in the studio is actually affected. It then opens into a large diameter of three feet. It is so stunning and unbelievable to everyone in the room that the reporter collapses, and passes out on the floor. Several chairs get toppled over, as crew and cameraman try to leave the studio. Another slender-female reporter trips over cords on the floor, while trying to run out of the room. There is a tremendous amount of chaos, and others still cannot believe what is happening.

Unfortunately, they are unable to get out of the studio. Suddenly walking up and out from this void is Captain Meyers. Everyone in the room is too stunned to respond. The captain heads to the table that is set up for the reporters, as the cameras are still rolling. He does not identify himself, but takes a seat.

He begins, announcing publicly to the world, his devastating plan and the new-technological war occurring.

He opens with the statement: "There is an incredible-technological upheaval that no human will be able to stop." The news instantly sparks a wave-of-terror, and the image of the captain travels quickly throughout the entire world. Some people watching Screenview begin to shout, while others state that the captain's words are incredulous. Many networks are interrupted to broadcast this unbelievable news. The captain continues: "There is going to be a huge-technological display of power. Some of it so subtle, no one will suspect or notice anything until it is too late." He warns: "Over the next-several days and weeks, more strange events will begin to occur everywhere, worldwide. This is all due, in part of a discovery that was made by one of your astronomers, Harve Ryan. Some time ago, an alien substance was found in your solar system."

Those remaining in the studio, although terrified, become angry. They wonder why this alien substance has never been made public. Viewers in their homes, and elsewhere hearing this awful news, are in total disbelief. Jim Harrison is also watching, and is practically out of his mind it utter shock. It takes him a while to gather his wits, and gain some sense of composure. He now understands the strange feeling he has had about the captain. His mind races with thoughts and images. He says aloud: "This can't be true. It's unreal. I've been working with him and he's..."

Amongst the disbelief, fear, and dread he's feeling, he has enough hatred left within him to do more harm. Jim uses this new-found knowledge to his advantage, and he communicates with the studio. He speaks with a man who's working in a room, a few doors down from where all of the chaos is taking place. The man listens to the defamatory statements being said, and takes note. The voice says: "My name is Jim Harrison, and I used to work with the astronomer. I had to end our working relationship, as he has lied to me and the world. He knew the dangers his discovery would cause. I also work with the man that is in your studio speaking, who is being seen all over the world. With him, I felt my life was in danger, so I went into hiding. I had to end our working relationship, as I found out he is an untrustworthy and manipulative man. I know all about the two of them. I tried to warn everyone." The man in the room keeps his eyes on the studio, in case he has to run for his safety. He whispers to Jim: "You should report this to the authorities. This is a very brave thing that you are doing, and you may be seen as a hero. Whatever information you have may help this situation."

The captain continues: "I have been housing this substance at DUG which your scientists have named Element

G. My purpose for housing this substance is to keep track of my race, and yours. This is done by using Element G as a communication, and tracking device in planning this technological upheaval." He says with a sly smile: "This substance uses cells. Cell-by-cell communication is faster than any communication device throughout the universe. It has become so simple and beneficial using it here. This type of communication is so fast that it travels at the speed of thought. I have learned how to use these cells. I can travel, and contact my kind at various times, while none of your people knew any of this. I am from the Virgo Cluster. The others, which I communicate with, are from other galaxies. They're millions of miles into space, and Element G is the ultimate tool making connection possible. We can contact each other instantaneously, whether in danger or otherwise. This is what makes Element G so powerful and useful by your kind and mine. I have realized that your kind will improperly manage its use. I am able to use it because, we have devices that are similar to what is being used here, and it has been incorporated into my cells. It is something that does not need further development. It should not be used in unconventional ways, thinking this is how it works. Scientists are only aware of certain aspects of its properties. They will not be able to produce any results through ongoing studies and tests. It is intelligent, and mutates. I have been aware of it for some time, and made it detectable to your scientists."

He again smiles and says: "That discovery has ruined everything for all of you. It makes retaliation impossible. Also, humans are weak minded, and will turn against one another." As he rises from his chair he says: "You cannot save yourselves without betraying one another. This, in turn, will pave the way for disaster. No one will be able to stop this."

After receiving numerous communications from a terrified public, a group of well-armed authority officers burst into the studio. They try to apprehend the captain. As they lift their weapons and begin to fire, they are prevented. The area of the studio surrounding him, again, makes a rumbling noise, then distorts wrapping around him. It forms a void that he walks into and disappears.

The female reporter on the floor becomes conscious. As medical help arrives, they take her from the studio. All the while, this is all caught on camera. Everyone viewing believes they are seeing the apocalypse. The authorities leave, as a male reporter apprehensively enters from a nearby room. He looks around to see if the area is safe. He is holding the information given to him that was sent in by Jim Harrison. It is the information he will be reporting.

The remaining-camera technicians put him on air, right where he's standing. As he relays the information, Jim

217

contacts Harve Ryan. He asks him menacingly: "Aren't you sorry now that you made this discovery you bastard? Now the whole world knows it's your fault, and you're the cause of all of this. Vengeance is sweet and it's all mine!"

As the news is now everywhere, an event is also happening on the East Coast.

At 4:45 p.m., a woman is standing on a busy-street corner at East 60th Street in Manhattan. She is with her beautiful, tan and brown, mixed-breed Cocker Spaniel. As the ground signal displays, they both hurry along to get to their Park Avenue apartment.

The dog pulls ahead of her, as if chasing something. She begins to hear a sound like scraping, and grinding rock from beneath the street. Her dog begins to growl at a manhole cover, and drags her close to it. As she pulls the dog across the street, the ground begins to make a moaning and rumbling noise. Everyone in the area thinks it's an earthquake, and run in different directions. There are howling sounds coming through the holes of the manhole cover.

The woman is alarmed, thinking she will soon see a worker emerge. Her dog yelps, and pulls her safely to the corner across the street. People curiously congregate at opposite corners, looking at the street. Then, suddenly there is a loud boom and there is an implosion in the middle of the street. The manhole cover gets pulled underground, leaving a gaping hole. Steam erupts, and vehicles get knocked back and cannot move. People begin running and screaming in every direction.

Back on the West Coast in San Francisco, the Golden Gate Bridge has begun to show signs of distress. Many buildings and homes in the surrounding-outer areas are also affected. They all have had repairs, or materials applied that have been incorporated with Element G. The bridge sways, as if by a strong wind or approaching storm. There is no apparent wind, or any known-external forces.

The water beneath the bridge becomes choppy, and various-large whirlpools can be seen swirling around. People in their vehicles feel trapped by the swaying, and some become panicked and screams are heard. Buildings and homes experience small rumbles, as though an earthquake is beginning. This lasts for about twenty seconds, and then completely stops

Then, suddenly, the bridge shakes violently and vehicle's crash into each other, causing many injuries. Many houses are damaged and various-outer sections have cracks and chips. Some shift off of their foundations and fall into the water below, as many pieces are pulled into the whirlpools.

Emergency units are dispersed, arriving at the bridge by boat away from the whirlpools. Videocopters and air vehicles are used for rescue. The news spread quickly, and is immediately classified as an alien invasion by black holes. Other events have begun to take place on other bridges. Also affected are railways, monuments, and installations. Homes are being affected in various ways. There are reports of meltdowns of railway stations, and buildings suddenly toppling. Strange objects are now being seen throughout the world, day and night.

A strange area on the West Coast has been uncovered by TC and his staff. With various scientists and other-organized groups they are looking for underground work stations, where the captain and Jim can hide. They find an abandoned-underground shelter stretching from San Bernardino to San Diego. One huge section in San Bernardino is not sealed off. TC and the secret authority raid the area looking for signs of life. They discover an enormous area that may have been part of a city onto itself. There are many strange findings, and other things that they cannot explain. One section, apparently, goes underground for miles. It has its own collection of oddities stored in what appears to be a warehouse-style museum.

Along a wall that extends into a very long hall, are images and illustrations that appear like genetically-altered human beings. There is a small-scale model of a white building with a flashing-purple chevron on the side. There are colossal amounts of unknown technology, and items that seem like weapons stored in various locations. Layouts and design plans of ideas are spread out on the ground, and other interesting sights. Somehow, all human personnel seem to have vanished or relocated. Left behind is an enormous array of technology. There is an eerie atmosphere within this area that is disturbing like that of a tomb.

As the scientist and secret authority continue to search around, they are suddenly struck with fear. Off in the distance, they peer into something very dark. It seems to be moving as if receding, and similar to looking into interstellar space. Not equipped for protecting themselves for what it could be, or what may be beyond, they go no further. Feeling incredibly uncomfortable at this site, they scurry back out into the warm daylight to the safety of higher ground.

As they emerge, TC says: "I think this is part of DUG that was never completed or its starting point. They all head to

221

San Diego to look for the white building with the Chevron on the side.

CHAPTER 9

Within the next couple of weeks, numerous, unidentified-flying object sightings are reported. Since the strange occurrences began on the West Coast, structural deterioration has become rampant. Across the states, buildings, landmarks, and public areas are taking on strange characteristics and functionality. Products and various devices are doing the same.

Throughout the United States, people and places begin to unravel. There are widespread disasters to airlines, and various modes of transportation. Partially constructed and other buildings have collapsed, trapping people inside and injuring many. There are no warnings prior to these events. It seems that Element G is to blame for these horrendous incidents.

Worldwide, the news headlines are all filled with the same horror. Many fear it may cripple the entire globe. All that is talked about is the end-of-the world. There are images everywhere of proclaimed flying saucers, and other supernatural and unexplained events. People everywhere are afraid of being in their homes, as well as leaving their homes. Other reports are from individuals stating that unseen forces and dimensions were abducting others.

On September 18th, the media reports have become more disturbing. In addition to the disappearance of the captain, Jim, and the missing computers, there is concern about a storm. Scientists have expressed concerned about the current, and unusual solar activity occurring on the sun. It has never been this powerful in known history, and there is a partial-solar eclipse occurring on September 21st. They are closely monitoring the flares, and any disturbances that may arise.

At 11:00 a.m. on the morning of September 19th, there are now reports of several power outages along the West Coast. There are also reports in The Mid-West, and throughout the Northeast. As the solar activity increases, many are quite fearful that the authorities will not be able to protect them. While the flares continue, a strange calm begins taking over the United States.

Suddenly, and without warning, the destruction abates and the strange sightings and occurrences cease. Over the next couple of days, the survivors of this awful destruction, and display of power try to move forward. They try to put the pieces back together of what was once their lives.

Many are still remembering the news reports about what the captain stated. The betrayal that has begun and those left behind having to fend for themselves. As anticipated, some are stealing from others because of fear of not surviving. Some are caught and imprisoned. Others have disappeared and are never heard from or seen again, as they cannot be identified.

Scientist's worldwide begin to rally together to devise what type of retaliation strategy to put into place. At 12:15 p.m., TC and his staff of scientist's are on their way to DUG. They are trying to decipher if the solar storm has cause the slowdown of occurrences. He brainstorms which action they should take to prevent this terrible happening from continuing. They are joined by the secret authority, and many other secret agencies putting together an incredible plan.

As TC leads the discussion, he believes that there is a cosmic correlation, and little time to act. He says: "I believe the solar flares are interrupting the activity that has been occurring. Everything seemed to have slowed down since the flares began. If we can have the states polarize their power supply, it will create a magnetic-energy field. It might interfere with all of this disaster that is occurring, and make it stop. One of his scientists interjects: "So we need to create a magnetic storm?" TC replies: "Yes, and a big one. I have another thought; maybe, the solar storm can take care of this on its own. If people have begun getting ill when visiting these new

225

medical facilities, that could possibly be where this began. We can only observe, and watch media reports of the latest developments.

Unknown to all, Captain Meyers has re-entered the laboratory and research building. He has summoned Jim to meet him there immediately. With all of the events taking place, the authorities have not put much emphasis on locating them. He knows no one would look for him at the laboratory, and it is a great hiding place over the weekend.

Being contacted by the captain, Jim is terrified to hear from him. He fears the actions he has taken and what he has said about him. The captain assures him that he's not in any danger, and he doesn't have any choice. Jim's mind and heart is racing. He is remembering what he said about the captain. Now, he may become just as guilty as Harve for following the captain. He wants to wash his hands of it all, and be free of any association to any wrongdoing. It won't be fruitful.

At 12:30 p.m., Jim meets the captain at the laboratory, and they head to DUG. On their way, the captain discusses their need to secure an area to safely work. They plan what else needs to be done. All the while, the captain seems to be behaving strangely, as if he is in imminent danger.

TC and his group, along with hoards of investigators, and secret authorities find D.U.G. As they begin their raid, they are awestruck to find that it is enormous. As the workers inside observe the intrusion, they are not fearful. They do not say a word. The authorities walk through several areas of this amazing marvel. They find they have bitten off more than they can chew. Venturing further, they find another world underground that's far beyond their expectations.

At 1:18 p.m., the captain and Jim arrive at DUG. They are not told of the authorities who are already there. Ironically, they head in the same direction as TC, and hear voices coming from a laboratory in front of them. Suddenly, the captain sees TC, and tries to escape leaving Jim behind. He is pursued by TC's group and is cornered. He realizes he can no longer escape through the void, as the cosmic occurrence is interfering with Element G. Also, some of the newly-built medical facilities have begun to ignite, and burn to the ground.

For the first time, he is apprehended by the authorities. They are unnerved to find the captain is incredibly light for a man of his stature. The captain and Jim are removed from DUG, and brought back to the laboratory and research building. They are placed in closed quarters and under surveillance. Over the weekend, they will be questioned

227

extensively. The media is not informed of this, for fear of causing another-public frenzy.

On Sunday, September 21st, the solar eclipse begins, and the solar-flare activity subsides. As it does, an enormous amount of unidentified-flying objects begin appearing worldwide in the sky. They are seen in various cities, and states, but stay at the same location. At every location where these objects appear, they move very slowly. They're not heading in any particular direction, or to any particular place. These objects do not seem to have any destination. In the daytime, these UFO's appear as small, round-dark objects. At nightfall, they appear as two, eerie-pink lights against a dark sky.

During the eclipse, the strange occurrences and sensations that have plagued so many have returned. It is now affecting the remaining medical facilities. Strange-pink lights are seen above, and circling around them. Although, they are no longer receiving patients, they continue to do damage in a variety of ways. Now all eyes are on the skies, and the surrounding areas. Nearby buildings and structures show signs of stress, and deterioration.

As more authoritative might is dispersed, air vehicles are surveying these sightings. They are also along waterways, and on land.

The public believes that the solar flares have temporarily thwarted these occurrences. Now that the sun is partially blocked, everything has resumed.

While all of this is taking place, Jim and the captain are placed in a briefing room. They are each bound, and tagged. They cannot escape, or move about freely. As they are detained here, more authority personnel arrive.

They are questioned by Authority Leader, Harold Wasser from the Authority of Investigations. Harold is surrounded by armed security, and is not afraid of the captain. He asks: "Who are you and what do you want?" Jim with fear written all over his face, believes the captain is powerless. He interjects Harold by saying: "He forced me into this. I told him I didn't want any part of it." The captain stares at Jim, coldly, without saying a word. Jim tries to continue, but Harold continues questioning the captain.

With the eclipse, and now aerial sightings, this has caused new fears. TC and his staff, along with other authority enforcement now handle the current-crisis situation. It is now blown-wide open. Those coming to assist are from various sects, they fill the skies, the ground and the waters. They interact with the general public, who fearfully believe, this will become part of their normal-daily lives.

Flyers in their air vehicles realize the unidentified-flying objects may be unearthly, and interdimensional. They are unsure as to how to pursue. The first-lead flyer slowly approaches one of the objects, and reports back to his superior. He says with alarm in his voice: "The object is something black, with a face and eyes." His superior responds back, "What did you say?" The flyer answers: "It's black with two pink eyes at and it looks…" He pauses for five seconds and says, "Frightening."

Suddenly, the objects eyes begin to illuminate with a bright-pink glow that terrifies the flyer. His voice raises and he says: "I think it is going to attack!" Suddenly the flyer fires at the object, but it goes straight through never touching it. He checks his panel to make sure that the object is appearing on his screen, and is not just his imagination. The object quickly passes, and encircles him. It still appears on his screen, and it is in front of him again. He is terrified, and fires at it again. This time the object disappears, and he cannot locate it. He reports back saying: "It's as though it's on a different plane, but appears like an object. There is nothing that I can physically destroy. It's like an image projected into the sky from some unknown place."`

At the same time, the population is trying to get as much information, as possible, about what is going on.

The flyer continues to search for the strange object, but it seems to have escaped. He communicates back: "I seem to have lost it. It no longer appears anywhere." His superior asks: "Tell me, again, what it looked like?" He responds: "It was oval shaped, and completely black. There were two-pink eyes made out of some casing. The eyes turned pink before I fired at it. It seems to have some type of base that supported it, but, I could not find any means for its operation. It must be some sort of alien-antigravity devise." His superior demands, "Okay! Report back to base." He responds, "Yes, sir!"

These incidents leave many on edge. There doesn't seem to be any functionality of these UFO's in regards to their positioning. Nonetheless, it is menacing and unsettling. Many people on the West Coast, through the East Coast, stay in their homes after dark. They are too afraid of this strange-atmospheric phenomenon. They try to follow the instructions of the authorities, but many have fallen apart.

At 9:00 p.m. on the East Coast, it is a clear-fall evening in Manhattan. Some men and women-adventure seekers are taking a ferry ride on the East River. As they sail along smoothly, there is something dark in the water. It catches the eye of one of the men. He points it out to the others and asks, "What's that?" Another man answers: "It's just a large buoy floating on the water."

The first man responds: "No, that's not a buoy. Look it's hovering. It isn't even in the water." Becoming apprehension he says, "I think it's coming towards us." Suddenly the dark image gets closer, and an outline of its shape can be seen by everyone. The boat operator tries to steer the ferry away, but two-pink eyes are now seen by everyone. Screams and chaos ensues, that are heard by other sailing vehicles on the water.

Suddenly, there is a very-bright pink flash. There are loud-crackling and popping sounds, and flames. The ferry is now only debris on the water with charred-bodies scattered about.

Witnesses communicate for help. Volunteers, and patrol boats immediately head to the area, and it is a grim sight.

Back in California, Harold Wasser questioning continues. He wants to know how the same object in the sky is seen everywhere simultaneously. The captain responds carefully: "It seems to be Eyesic and Rfactor, and they may have become one. Being that they are cloning computers, they are doing what they believe they're designed to do. I don't know for sure, if that is the case, or how it is done. It seems as though it's cloning its image to instill fear."

Harold informs his people to alert the public about the objects in the sky. The public is then informed by the media. They are told that these terrifying sightings may just be cloned images of the missing computers. This information is even more terrifying, as no one knows if some of the objects are real or unreal.

At this very moment, the objects across the skies begin to move about more quickly. It's as though, they're planning a simultaneous attack.

Similar images from the sky begin appearing on the streets on the East Coast. They also appear above some low and high-rise buildings. Some of the images begin to blast pink-energy laser on people in parks, and in vehicles. People run and hide everywhere they can, and the sky becomes filled with air vehicles. They try to dispel the chaos, by trying to somehow destroy the images. The situation is terrible, as there is so much uncertainty and so much fear.

Harold then receives information about the ferry incident on the East Coast. He explodes with anger and starts yelling: "Many people on the East Coast have just been killed by something. What evil have you brought upon us? Don't tell me this happened from an image. It is clearly something real!" The captain is hesitant to answer, and Harold explosively demands, "How do we stop this apocalypse?" As the captain rises from his chair, security draws their weapons. Harold continues: "Tell us right now how to stop this. If you don't, I'll kill you!" Jim is terrified, and looks to the captain for answers. The captain not wanting to be killed, and unable to escape reluctantly answers: "There is only one who knows, and he can...!"

Suddenly, a black void opens on the floor right next to the captain. He realizes his escaping ability has returned. Just as he jumps up and tries to flee, Harold yells, "Fire!" Jim ducks to the side, as shots are fired into the captain. There are three shots fired in succession that resonate throughout the room. They are ear-piercing explosions. Boom! Boom! Boom!

These loud sounds of shots being fired are also heard in the ears of someone who is in a deep sleep. He is startled and awakened by the noise. It is Paul DeAngelo, the scientist who had been lying asleep in his bed. Before awakening, he believes he is hearing the sounds of explosions. He remembers someone being shot in his dream. When he comes to his senses, he soon realizes that TC is standing over his bed, and has knocked three times on his headboard.

Paul is quite startled, and bolts straight up in bed blurting out: "There was an explosion. Someone got shot!" TC looks at him strangely and says: "It was probably me knocking on the headboard just now to wake you up. It must have coincided with what you were dreaming about. Hey man, when you left work early on Thursday, and didn't come in on Friday, I got concerned. I figured you needed more time to catch up on the errands you were doing. There was no communication from you after that. I didn't say anything to anyone, and covered for you. I had to leave town for a couple of days, and left you a few messages on your Screenview. I didn't get back into town until late Sunday evening, so we took it upon ourselves to come and see about you. We decided to come first thing today, Monday, since we haven't heard from you. Your vehicle is still at the laboratory. How did you get home?"

Paul says shakily and sleepily: "But I heard the explosion, and they were shots." TC replies: "There were no shots. What are you talking about? You have been dreaming."

Paul straightens himself up on the bed and says groggily: "No! This was no dream! I had this solution, and it spilled on my jacket. I had this strange encounter in my vehicle. I went back to the laboratory to return it. When I got home, I felt something had happened to me. I fell asleep afterwards, and I cannot seem to remember anything else." TC has a very shocked and surprised expression on his face. He is not sure what to make of the strange dream.

Paul is now completely awake and continues: "There were these computers we were working on, and this technology. Then there was this alien takeover. The computers were supposed to help people, but something happened. The captain was in charge of everything, and he held me captive. You have to help me! He is going to get me!" He continues to ramble, but then stops and thinks. Then he says: "We have to destroy those computers, and I know how. I was shown how. The sun, we have to use the sun during an eclipse and..."

TC just stares as Paul continues: "Those shots I heard were for the captain, and he was trying to escape. He was shot and could have been killed." He exclaims with passion, "You have to believe me. The captain may be dead!" Then he abruptly stops himself and realizes what TC said earlier. He then asks: "What do you mean, we took it upon ourselves to come here? Who are we?"

TC looks at him apprehensively and says: "Well, I wanted to stop you before you went on with your fantastic story. He's coming now through the living room." Just then, TC yells from the bedroom: "He's in here, and he's alright!"

Before another word is spoken, Paul nervously begins to slide back down on the bed. He is trying to make sense of this sensational happening. When he looks up, he is mortified and his lips begin to quiver. Bolting up, he slams his head on the headboard. He grows pale and starts shaking, and his mouth flies open. TC excitedly asks, "Oh my God, Paul, what's wrong?"

Strutting in with a sinister grin from ear-to-ear is Captain Meyers. Paul notices three-small tears in his uniform. One tear is directly in his chest, one on his right shoulder, and the other on his left forearm. TC can also see this, and now understands Paul's fear.

TC and Paul are motionless, and filled with fear and dread. They just stare at the captain in disbelief and shock. The captain deviously says to Paul: "The last time I heard from you, you were at the laboratory. Well, that's where I need you now; there's a big experiment that is going to take place…"

THE END….

ABOUT THE COVER

As the author, Susan Varo has also created the cover for the book The Happening. This incredible and indelible illustration portrays a chilling and sinister moment from within the book, when chaos fills the skies. The world gets to see the face of the terrifying menace that has been unleased onto the world pursuing woman and mankind with some unknown catastrophic plan.

Made in the USA
Middletown, DE
27 May 2017